CASHMERE CONSPIRACY

(A Hazel Stitchworth Cozy Mystery—Book One)

FIONA GRACE

Fiona Grace

Fiona Grace is author of the LACEY DOYLE COZY MYSTERY series, comprising nine books; of the TUSCAN VINEYARD COZY MYSTERY series, comprising seven books; of the DUBIOUS WITCH COZY MYSTERY series, comprising three books; of the BEACHFRONT BAKERY COZY MYSTERY series, comprising six books; of the CATS AND DOGS COZY MYSTERY series, comprising nine books; of the ELIZA MONTAGU COZY MYSTERY series, comprising nine books (and counting); of the ENDLESS HARBOR ROMANTIC COMEDY series, comprising nine books (and counting); of the INN AT DUNE ISLAND ROMANTIC COMEDY series, comprising seven books (and counting); of the INN BY THE SEA ROMANTIC COMEDY series, comprising five books (and counting); of the MAID AND THE MANSION COZY MYSTERY series, comprising five books (and counting); of the ALICE BLOOM COZY MYSTERY series, comprising five books (and counting); of the MAGNOLIA BAY COZY MYSTERY series, comprising five books (and counting); of the TIMBERLAKE TITANS HOCKEY ROMANCE series, comprising five books (and counting); of the ASHVILLE ACES HOCKEY ROMANCE series, comprising five books (and counting); of the PENNY HAWTHORNE cozy mystery series, comprising seven books (and counting); and of the DELILAH GREEN cozy mystery series, comprising five books (and counting).

Fiona would love to hear from you, so please visit www.fionagraceauthor.com to receive free ebooks, hear the latest news, and stay in touch.

ISBN: 978-1-0943-8800-7

BOOKS BY FIONA GRACE

DELILAH GREEN COZY MYSTERY
ORCHID OBSESSION (Book #1)
LETHAL LEAVES (Book #2)
BETRAYAL IN BLOOM (Book #3)
SINISTER SEEDS (Book #4)
FATAL FOLIAGE (Book #5)

PENNY HAWTHORNE COZY MYSTERY
HERBAL HOMICIDE (Book #1)
VANILLA VENDETTA (Book #2)
PEPPERMINT PERIL (Book #3)
MINTY MALICE (Book #4)
CHAMOMILE CALAMITY (Book #5)
FENNEL FATALITY (Book #6)
EARL GREY ALIBI (Book #7)

ASHVILLE ACES HOCKEY ROMANCE
BREAKAWAY BLISS (Book #1)
ICY INTIMACY (Book #2)
FACEOFF FLING (Book #3)
RINK RENDEZVOUS (Book #4)
HOCKEY HEARTTHROB (Book #5)

TIMBERLAKE TITANS HOCKEY ROMANCE
RINKSIDE ROMANCE (Book #1)
FLIRTY FACEOFF (Book #2)
MELTING THE ICE (Book #3)
THE PUCK STOPS HERE (Book #4)
GLOVES DROP, LOVE BLOOMS (Book #5)

MAGNOLIA BAY COZY MYSTERY
THE TAINTED TAFFY (Book #1)
A MASKED MURDER (Book #2)
A CAFE CONFESSION (Book #3)
THE FROZEN FIND (Book #4)
A CURIOUS CURSE (Book #5)

TIMBERLAKE TITANS HOCKEY ROMANCE
RINKSIDE ROMANCE (Book #1)
FLIRTY FACEOFF (Book #2)
MELTING THE ICE (Book #3)
THE PUCK STOPS HERE (Book #4)
GLOVES DROP, LOVE BLOOMS (Book #5)

ALICE BLOOM COZY MYSTERY
MURDER IN THE MARIGOLDS (Book #1)
RUIN IN THE ROSES (Book #2)
DECEIT IN THE DAFFODILS (Book #3)
SCANDAL IN THE SAFFRON (Book #4)
CATASTROPHE IN THE CARNATIONS (Book #5)

THE MAID AND THE MANSION COZY MYSTERY
A MYSTERIOUS MURDER (Book #1)
A SCANDALOUS DEATH (Book #2)
A MISSING GUEST (Book #3)
AN UNSOLVABLE CRIME (Book #4)
AN IMPOSSIBLE HEIST (Book #5)

INN BY THE SEA ROMANTIC COMEDY
A NEW LOVE (Book #1)
A NEW CHANCE (Book #2)
A NEW HOME (Book #3)
A NEW LIFE (Book #4)
A NEW ME (Book #5)

THE INN AT DUNE ISLAND ROMANTIC COMEDY
A CHANCE LOVE (Book #1)
A CHANCE FALL (Book #2)
A CHANCE ROMANCE (Book #3)
A CHANCE CHRISTMAS (Book #4)
A CHANCE ENGAGEMENT (Book #5)
A CHANCE DREAM (Book #6)
A CHANCE WEDDING (Book #7)

ENDLESS HARBOR ROMANTIC COMEDY
ALWAYS, WITH YOU (Book #1)
ALWAYS, FOREVER (Book #2)
ALWAYS, PLUS ONE (Book #3)

ALWAYS, TOGETHER (Book #4)
ALWAYS, LIKE THIS (Book #5)
ALWAYS, FATED (Book #6)
ALWAYS, FOR LOVE (Book #7)
ALWAYS, JUST US (Book #8)
ALWAYS, IN LOVE (Book #9)

ELIZA MONTAGU COZY MYSTERY
MURDER AT THE HEDGEROW (Book #1)
A DALLOP OF DEATH (Book #2)
CALAMITY AT THE BALL (Book #3)
A SPEAKEASY DEMISE (Book #4)
A FLAPPER FATALITY (Book #5)
BUMPED BY A DAME (Book #6)
A DOLL'S DEBACLE (Book #7)
A FELLA'S RUIN (Book #8)
A GAL'S OFFING (Book #9)

LACEY DOYLE COZY MYSTERY
MURDER IN THE MANOR (Book#1)
DEATH AND A DOG (Book #2)
CRIME IN THE CAFE (Book #3)
VEXED ON A VISIT (Book #4)
KILLED WITH A KISS (Book #5)
PERISHED BY A PAINTING (Book #6)
SILENCED BY A SPELL (Book #7)
FRAMED BY A FORGERY (Book #8)
CATASTROPHE IN A CLOISTER (Book #9)

TUSCAN VINEYARD COZY MYSTERY
AGED FOR MURDER (Book #1)
AGED FOR DEATH (Book #2)
AGED FOR MAYHEM (Book #3)
AGED FOR SEDUCTION (Book #4)
AGED FOR VENGEANCE (Book #5)
AGED FOR ACRIMONY (Book #6)
AGED FOR MALICE (Book #7)

DUBIOUS WITCH COZY MYSTERY
SKEPTIC IN SALEM: AN EPISODE OF MURDER (Book #1)
SKEPTIC IN SALEM: AN EPISODE OF CRIME (Book #2)

SKEPTIC IN SALEM: AN EPISODE OF DEATH (Book #3)

BEACHFRONT BAKERY COZY MYSTERY
BEACHFRONT BAKERY: A KILLER CUPCAKE (Book #1)
BEACHFRONT BAKERY: A MURDEROUS MACARON (Book #2)
BEACHFRONT BAKERY: A PERILOUS CAKE POP (Book #3)
BEACHFRONT BAKERY: A DEADLY DANISH (Book #4)
BEACHFRONT BAKERY: A TREACHEROUS TART (Book #5)
BEACHFRONT BAKERY: A CALAMITOUS COOKIE (Book #6)

CATS AND DOGS COZY MYSTERY
A VILLA IN SICILY: OLIVE OIL AND MURDER (Book #1)
A VILLA IN SICILY: FIGS AND A CADAVER (Book #2)
A VILLA IN SICILY: VINO AND DEATH (Book #3)
A VILLA IN SICILY: CAPERS AND CALAMITY (Book #4)
A VILLA IN SICILY: ORANGE GROVES AND VENGEANCE (Book #5)
A VILLA IN SICILY: CANNOLI AND A CASUALTY (Book #6)

CHAPTER ONE

Hazel Stitchworth perched on a wooden stool that had seen better days, its creaks harmonizing with the soft strum of acoustic music that wafted through The Knitter's Nook. Her fingers danced nimbly over the emerging sweater, coaxing the wool into interlocking loops and patterns. Around her, the shop was a cozy mixture of texture and hue, with skeins of yarn crowding the shelves in an artist's palette of colors. Chunky blues mingled with delicate pinks, while threads of greens and purples promised endless possibilities to the discerning eye.

"Fiona, did you manage to crunch those numbers yet?" Hazel called out without looking up from her project, her voice as comfortable in the space as the familiar click of knitting needles.

Fiona Mackenzie, ensconced behind the counter amidst a fortress of receipts and financial statements, didn't miss a beat with her calculator. Hazel adored her best friend's ability to take care of the business side while she took care of the inventory. "Still wading through this sea of bills," she replied, the red numbers on the calculator display flickering like a lighthouse in fog. "I'll have your treasure chest total soon."

Hazel huffed a laugh, her hands never pausing. "Treasure chest, huh? I'm hoping for more of a war chest. That festival won't know what hit it."

The shop seemed to hold its breath with her, every spool of yarn and knitting needle waiting in silent camaraderie for Fiona's final tally.

Hazel let out a wistful sigh, her gaze shifting from the complicated pattern of the half-finished sweater to the tranquility of her shop. The Knitter's Nook was a sanctuary of softness, each shelf bearing the weight of yarns as diverse as the leaves in autumn. She could practically feel the textures with her eyes - wool that whispered of cozy winter evenings and silks that gleamed like morning dew.

"Sometimes," she mused aloud, "I think I'd rather be tangled up in bills than in these stitches." She eyed the tiny gap in her work where the stitches had slipped away like mischievous sprites.

Fiona glanced over, her fingers never stopping their dance across the calculator keys. "Why not unravel it and start something new? Seems like that sweater is giving you a fit. It's not the first time you've complained about it. You're probably going to drop more stitches, why not cut your losses?"

Hazel looked up, her expression sketched with mock horror. "Abandon ship halfway through the storm? Fiona Mackenzie, you wound me!"

"Most folks don't cling to a sinking ship just for the view," Fiona quipped, not lifting her eyes from the stream of numbers on her screen.

"Perfectionism isn't a crime," Hazel retorted, her needles clicking in mild frustration. "I want it flawless."

"Gosh, I feel like you grow more stubborn every day," Fiona declared with an affectionate roll of her eyes as she finally set aside the calculator. She gathered a printed sheet from the cluttered counter and carried it over to Hazel, who rested her knitting in her lap to accept the paper. "This is your budget for the European Fiber Festival. Spend wisely, my friend."

The numbers and figures swam before Hazel's eyes as she scanned the document, the promise of exotic yarns from distant lands already spinning in her head. She allowed herself a small, satisfied nod. "I can work with this."

"Remember, 'necessities' don't include every shade of blue they have," Fiona teased, her smile evident in her voice.

"Only the ones I don't have yet," Hazel replied, a conspiratorial twinkle lighting up her eyes as she picked up her needles once more, determined to conquer the rebellious stitches.

Hazel's smile grew as she thought about her upcoming trip. "This should be just the ticket to snag my usual cache of cashmere and maybe even a skein of that merino I've been eyeing," she mused aloud, the prospect of new yarns weaving a sense of excitement through her.

"Keep it within those margins, Hazel, and we'll be doing well for ourselves this month," Fiona reminded her, the corners of her lips twitching upwards.

"Where would I be without you?" Hazel chuckled, setting down the budget sheet as if it were a treasure map leading to yarn-filled X marks. "Probably buried under a mountain of yarn with no business and no friends."

"Exactly, and I'd rather not excavate you from an avalanche of angora blends," Fiona shot back, her tone light but her gaze serious. The calculator clicked as she tucked it away, a silent sentinel ready for its next arithmetic battle.

Hazel picked up her knitting, the needles clicking like a metronome marking the rhythm of their conversation. "You know, you might have a point there," she conceded with a playful nod.

"Are your bags all set for Spain?" Fiona asked, tapping a pen against the counter as if mapping out Hazel's itinerary herself.

"Nearly there," Hazel replied, her fingers deftly catching a rogue stitch. "But I'll need to play a bit of suitcase Tetris to make room for the return haul of yarn. Otherwise, we'll be footing the bill for extra luggage."

"Pack smart, not heavy," Fiona advised, leaning against the counter. "You'll thank yourself when you're not sacrificing your splurge funds for baggage fees."

"I suppose I could always wear half my wardrobe on the plane," Hazel quipped, her imagination already running wild with the logistics of packing multiple layers. "Who needs comfort when you can have more yarn?"

"Practicality suits you, Hazel," Fiona said, her laughter mingling with the soft strains of music floating from the speakers. "Just remember, you're going to Spain, not the Arctic."

The two friends shared a knowing look, their bond as tightly knit as the patterns that filled the shop with color and life. With a final adjustment to her stitches, Hazel tucked her work into her bag, ready for whatever tangles awaited her abroad.

Hazel exhaled a wistful sigh. "You're probably right," she murmured, glancing up at Fiona with resignation. "I ought to go home and make some room in those bags. Besides, I still need to check in with Rosemary before I leave."

"Of course," Fiona replied, her voice steady like the anchor of their ship. "I'll keep the fort warm and the yarns turning here." The corners of her mouth lifted in a knowing smile.

"Again, where would I be without you?" Hazel said, half-rhetorical, her words tinted with the gratitude that had woven itself into the very foundation of their friendship.

"Probably tangled in a web of your own making, somewhere not nearly as cozy as this shop," Fiona quipped back, her eyes twinkling with shared history.

Hazel chuckled, slinging her knitting bag over her shoulder with a practiced ease. "Yeah, probably," she agreed, already picturing the chaos of yarns untamed by Fiona's meticulous care.

As she prepared to depart, Hazel's keen eye caught a glimpse of movement by the counter. Fiona was turning, her attention drawn to a space beneath it, unaware of the precarious position of a paper bag teetering on the edge. With the reflexes honed by countless saved stitches, Hazel darted forward, snagging the bag just as gravity declared its intentions.

"Whoa, thanks," Fiona exclaimed, her gaze snapping to the near-catastrophe. "That was close. It almost tipped over all of my meticulously sorted receipts."

"Always watching out for each other," Hazel remarked with a grin, setting the bag safely onto the counter.

"Seems like it's my turn to be in stitches," Fiona laughed, shaking her head at the close call.

Hazel chuckled softly, the corner of her mouth lifting in an amused smile. "You’re lucky I've got eyes like a hawk when it comes to impending yarn disasters," she said, watching Fiona with a mixture of concern and mirth dancing in her eyes. "Just keep your head above the wool, okay?"

"Promise I will," Fiona replied, tucking a stray strand of hair behind her ear as she met Hazel's gaze. "Now shoo! Spain won't wait and neither will those exclusive merino blends you've been dreaming about."

"True enough," Hazel agreed, giving a playful salute. "I'll call you later to check in. Make sure the shop doesn't unravel without me."

"Go on, get ready for another grand adventure. We’ve both got work to do," Fiona said, her voice tinged with both pride and a touch of mock seriousness.

With a final nod and a wave, Hazel turned on her heel and pushed open the door to The Knitter's Nook, stepping out into the embrace of Knotsville's warm air. The town greeted her with its usual charm, the afternoon sun casting a golden hue over the cobblestone streets that wound lazily through the quaint downtown area. Shopfronts boasted hand-painted signs, each one inviting passersby with the promise of unique local treasures—from the old-fashioned bakery with its ever-tempting scent of fresh bread to the tiny bookshop where stories waited to be discovered between well-loved pages.

As she strolled towards Rosemary's cozy inn, Hazel passed Mrs. Wentworth's flower shop, the vibrant blooms spilling onto the sidewalk in a riotous display of color and life. She waved to Mr. Jenkins, who was polishing his antique car, a labor of love he undertook every

Thursday without fail. Each familiar sight filled her with a sense of contentment; this was her world, where every stitch of community was interwoven with care.

A soft breeze ruffled her hair, carrying with it the mingled scents of lilac and freshly cut grass—a reminder that even as she prepared for international escapades, the simple pleasures of home were hard to rival. Hazel's steps were light, her heart already weaving the memories she would bring back to share, much like the intricate patterns she so lovingly crafted with her needles. She was excited to visit her sister, at the Inn she'd known her entire life.

CHAPTER TWO

Hazel pushed open the polished oak door of the Stitchworth Inn, the familiar chime singing out as she stepped into the warm embrace of history. The building, a stately Victorian structure complete with gabled roofs and intricate woodwork, had been a cornerstone of Knotsville for generations. Each corner of the lobby whispered tales of bygone eras, from the antique grandfather clock ticking away in the alcove to the original hardwood floors that creaked softly underfoot, telling stories with every step.

Her sister, Rosemary, was absorbed in her work, polishing the front table until it gleamed like a mirror beneath the honeyed glow of the overhead chandelier. Just beyond, Penny, the ever-cheerful front desk helper, was busy with a couple, likely charmed by the inn's historic allure, checking them into one of the cozy rooms upstairs.

"Rosemary," Hazel called out softly, prompting her sister to glance up.

Upon seeing Hazel, Rosemary's face lit up with a warmth that matched the hearth's flickering fire. She dashed around the table, sending a rogue feather duster twirling through the air, and enveloped Hazel in an eager hug. "Hello, you!" Rosemary beamed, her voice filled with the kind of affection that only siblings share.

"Hey there," Hazel chuckled, returning the hug before stepping back. "How's the inn doing?"

"Pretty well, actually," Rosemary said with a nod, releasing Hazel and smoothing down her apron adorned with a delicate floral pattern. Her eyes sparkled as she continued, "We're getting a lot of guests for some kind of major business convention a few towns over. Something about insurance."

"Sounds like you're pretty busy then." Hazel glanced at the couple Penny was assisting, who seemed delighted with their room keys.

"Busy? Yes," Rosemary replied with another nod, a faint laugh escaping her lips. "But not as chaotic as your life usually is." There was a hint of mischief in her tone, the kind that hinted at untold stories and the bustling energy that came with running the beloved family inn.

Hazel smiled, knowing all too well the controlled chaos that she thrived in, the festivals, the tours, the learning everything she can about fibers and yarn making.

"Chaotic? Hardly," Hazel replied with a dismissive wave of her hand, the silver charm bracelet on her wrist jingling softly. "I'm just a little tied up with a few things." She watched as Penny handed the couple a brass key, which glinted in the warm light filtering through the lace curtains. The couple walked towards their room, leaving the lobby empty of guests.

Rosemary's eyebrows arched slightly, her gaze locking onto Hazel's with sisterly scrutiny. "Isn't there a plane to Spain with your name on it?" she asked, leaning against the polished oak reception desk that had seen generations of guests come and go.

"Ah, yes, but that's all in a day's work," Hazel nodded, brushing a loose strand of hair behind her ear. "Just picking up my usual rare alpaca wool from a supplier at the European Fiber Festival. You know, the norm for a yarn connoisseur."

"Still sounds like quite the endeavor," Rosemary said, a smile tugging at the corners of her mouth. "Yet you're as unflappable as ever."

Hazel's lips curled into a smirk, and she gave an easy shrug. "It's just another Tuesday." She glanced sideways, following the couple with her eyes as they ascended the grand staircase, their footsteps muffled by the plush crimson carpet. "Of course, it's exciting. New places, new faces. But in reality, it's business as usual. I'm actually looking forward to some downtime—just me, shopping around, and maybe lounging in my hotel room with a good book."

"Anytime you need a change of scenery without crossing the ocean, you have an open invitation here," Rosemary offered warmly, gesturing to the surrounding walls that held countless memories within their time-worn bricks.

"Thanks, Rosie," Hazel responded, her tone carrying a mix of appreciation and playful sarcasm. "But I think I've memorized every creaky floorboard and cozy nook this place has to offer."

Their laughter mingled and lingered in the air, a testament to their shared history within the comforting embrace of the Stitchworth Inn. “That can’t be true,” Rosemary joked.

Hazel's chuckle reverberated softly against the Inn's antique fixtures as she mused aloud, "I reckon I've tested every mattress and fluffed every pillow in this place. But I'll remember to check in next time I'm in a stitch." She cast a glance at Rosemary, her eyes twinkling with the anticipation of shared amusement.

There was a silence between them before Hazel clarified, “Like a stitch, like a situation?” She smiled at her sister expectantly.

Rosemary's expression, however, was tinged with the subtle hue of melancholy. "Oh, Hazel," she began, her voice carrying the weight of unspoken words, "I get your puns. But you should probably head out. Isn't there a suitcase waiting for your expert packing skills?"

"True," Hazel conceded, a wistful sigh threading through her response. "I’m on strict orders to make room for all of my fibers or I won’t get to have any fun this week."

With an affectionate squeeze, Hazel wrapped her arms around Rosemary once more, the warmth between them palpable.

Pulling away, Hazel's gaze lingered on the familiar surroundings—the worn wooden floorboards whispering tales of bygone days, the gentle clink of china from the dining room where guests savored Rosemary's culinary delights. She turned towards the door, the brass handle cool under her touch.

"Safe travels," Rosemary called after her, her voice steady but not quite free of concern. "And don't forget to send me a message when you land. You know how I worry."

"Of course, Rosie," Hazel replied, casting a look over her shoulder that bridged the distance between them. "You'll be the first to know."

Stepping out of the Stitchworth Inn, Hazel felt the chapter of home close gently behind her, the latch clicking into place with a sound that signaled both an ending and a beginning. The door framed her departure like the final stitch in a well-crafted garment—neat, necessary, and leading to the next pattern to explore.

The sun laid its gentle caress on Hazel's cheeks as she strolled down the main street of Knotsville, the historic lamp posts standing like sentries along the cobblestone path. The quaint shops, with their awnings striped in faded pastels, nodded in the soft summer breeze, each window displaying a tableau of small-town life: handcrafted jewelry, freshly baked pies, and books with spines creased from countless readings.

Knotsville was a tapestry woven from threads of nostalgia and simplicity, where every brick seemed to whisper a story of the Stitchworth legacy. The air carried the scent of blooming wisteria, mingling with the faint aroma of coffee and old paper from the bookstore on the corner. Here, Hazel could always find solace in the familiar rhythm of local chatter and the chime of the antique store door.

Yet, as her steps fell into the comfortable cadence of home, Hazel's eyes caught sight of a figure approaching—a tall, broad-shouldered silhouette that struck a note of dissonance in the harmony of her day. It was Garrett Pearson, his posture radiating an eagerness that belied the badge pinned to his chest. Her ex-boyfriend was the last person she wanted to see right now.

Of all the roads in Knotsville, he has to walk into my path, and the timing... just great, Hazel thought to herself. She felt a warmth that had nothing to do with the sun's embrace or the knitted shawl draped over her shoulders—a residual heat from embers thought to be long extinguished.

Glancing left and then right, Hazel quickly realized that there was no convenient alley to dart into, no friend's shop door at which to feign urgent business. The open expanse of the town square offered no place of refuge, leaving her exposed under the scrutiny of Garrett's determined stride.

She felt momentarily ensnared in an invisible net, her feet betraying her by refusing to move in any direction that might offer escape. Her heart did a little two-step against her will, and Hazel scolded it silently for forgetting the choreography of moving on.

Act natural, she coached herself, *it's just a normal day*.

As if sensing her silent plea for invisibility, Garrett raised a hand in greeting, his smile reaching his blue eyes, those same eyes that had once mapped out constellations in her freckles. There was a familiarity in his gesture—a remnant of days when a raise of his hand would have been a prelude to an embrace.

"Steady, Hazel," she whispered, taking a deep breath. The sweet fragrance of wisteria filled her lungs, a reminder that even the loveliest blooms had thorns hidden beneath their beauty. With her hands swinging at her side, she prepared to face what she couldn't avoid, her legs twitching with the urge to run away.

Raising her hand with a slight tremor, Hazel acknowledged Garrett's presence. The sheepish gesture was as involuntary as a dropped stitch in her otherwise flawless knitting. She maintained a fixed smile, one that had more in common with a grimace, as she came face to face with the man whose uniform still seemed to fit him as snugly as their history did.

"Hey, Hazel," he started, his voice carrying the hopeful lilt of someone who hasn't read the last page of their story yet. "I'd love to talk."

"Actually, I'm just leaving," Hazel blurted out, words tumbling from her lips. "I have to get home so I can pack for a trip, so... bye now." The sentence ended on a high note, as if it were a question hanging by a thread in the air between them.

She turned briskly, the click of her heels on the sidewalk punctuating her departure. With one look back, she caught sight of Garrett's deflated stature, his hands sinking into his pockets as if trying to retrieve the conversation they never had.

As Hazel quickened her pace, she couldn't shake off the weight of unsaid words that seemed to follow her like shadows at sunset. She told herself she needed a longer list of excuses to avoid these run-ins with Garrett. Their relationship had unraveled months ago, and she wasn't eager to pick up those loose ends again.

"Focus on Spain," she whispered under her breath, imagining the vibrant threads of alpaca wool waiting for her, a tapestry of distractions from the life she had woven here. The festival ahead promised new patterns to explore, far removed from the familiar weave of Knotsville and the ties that still bound her to Garrett.

"Spain," she repeated, letting the word roll over her tongue like a secret promise. It was her lifeline, her escape from this small town where every corner turned into a potential rendezvous with memories she'd rather leave tucked away.

With each step, the sun warmed her face, and she felt the day's embrace. It was a gentle reminder that even when past loves loomed large on mainstreet sidewalks, there was always another horizon to chase, another skein of adventure to unravel.

CHAPTER THREE

Hazel nestled into the window seat, her gaze flitting between the clouds outside and the grid of symbols laid out on her notebook. The pencil in her hand tapped rhythmically against her cheek, a metronome for her thoughts as she contemplated her next move. With every symbol penciled into a square, the pattern beneath her fingertips slowly emerged, each stitch a step closer to the vision in her mind. It was shaping up to be intricate, possibly one of her most elaborate designs yet.

The hum of the plane's engine was a comforting backdrop to Hazel's concentration. However, the sound was momentarily overshadowed by the squeaky wheel of the beverage cart inching down the aisle. The flight attendant, sporting a practiced smile, paused beside Hazel's row.

"Would you like something to drink?" she offered cheerily.

Hazel barely glanced up from her design, shaking her head with a polite "No, thank you." Her focus was unbreakable; the pattern was calling to her, begging to be completed.

She heard the rustle of fabric next to her as the older woman settled back into her seat, a plastic cup of water in hand. "What's that you're working on there?" the woman inquired, peering over with a mix of curiosity and something else—was it bemusement?

The question gave Hazel the thrill of talking about something she loved, and she turned towards her neighbor with a warm smile. "Oh, it's a work project," she said, her voice tinged with the excitement of sharing her passion. "It's a knitting pattern."

The older woman nodded, taking a sip of her water, her interest piqued enough to put aside her magazine. Hazel held up the notebook, offering a glimpse into the world contained within those tiny squares—a world of texture, color, and endless possibilities.

"Each little square is a stitch," Hazel explained, her fingers tracing the grid of symbols as if they could already feel the texture of yarn between them. "And together, they'll form a cable knit pattern." She picked up her pencil once more, the graphite tip lightly tapping each symbol as she outlined the blueprint of her next creation.

The woman, whose eyes had been following Hazel's movements with a sharpness that belied her tranquil exterior, interjected with a chuckle, "You seem to know your way around a pair of knitting needles."

Hazel beamed at the comment, pride swelling in her chest. "Well, I should hope so—I own a store dedicated to it." She couldn't resist adding a little flourish to her confession, her hand sweeping grandly as though unveiling an invisible shopfront.

"Really? A whole store for knitting?" The older woman's eyebrows lifted in genuine surprise, and Hazel noticed a twinkle of intrigue in her eyes that hadn't been there before.

"Yes," Hazel affirmed, leaning back against the cushioned seat, the hum of the plane's engine a steady rhythm that somehow complemented her elevated mood. "It's a cozy little place, but it's pretty popular, in person and online. Knitting is for everyone, afterall."

Hazel took in the woman's attire, specifically the purple hat on her head. It looked like it was hand-made, artisanal, but Hazel couldn't be sure without touching it and she wasn't going to do that. Not with how this woman was already seeming to judge her, looking her up and down with those eyes.

That along with her age made Hazel wonder why the woman was so against knitting, when most women around her age loved the hobby, or had at the very least, heard of it. She didn't want to assume or make stereotypes, but she'd never heard of a woman being so negative about the hobby she loved.

Hazel offered a polite nod and mustered the warmest smile she could. "Yes, indeed. Knitter's Nook is its name," she said, her voice tinged with pride. The woman beside her let out a small, somewhat dismissive chuckle, raising an eyebrow in mock curiosity.

"And what, pray tell, does one sell in a knitting store?" the woman inquired, skepticism woven into her tone.

The question hung in the air for a moment, heavy and unwelcome, like a woolen blanket in summer. Hazel felt a familiar twinge of defensiveness clutch at her chest—she'd encountered this sort of attitude before. Yet, her passion for her craft always overruled any reluctance to share it. With a determined tilt of her chin, Hazel decided that no amount of scoffing would unravel her enthusiasm.

"Everything a knitter's heart might desire," Hazel began, her words cascading like yarn spilling from a basket. "Yarn in every shade you can imagine, from the softest pastels to the deepest jewel tones. Needles, patterns, and all manner of accessories."

"Right, well, that's nice," the older woman responded, her interest seeming to wane as she spoke, yet there was a glint of something—a hint of curiosity, perhaps—in her eye. Hazel wasn't done, though; she grabbed the thread of conversation and ran with it. Knowing that if the woman beside her was going to be annoyed by her, she might as well give her a reason to be.

"Knitting's quite popular, you know," Hazel continued, her hands gesturing as if she were casting on an invisible project. "It's not just about creating something beautiful or practical—it's about the joy of the process, the community. In my shop, we welcome everyone, from seasoned knitters to those just learning how to wield a pair of needles."

"Is that so?" The woman's tone remained noncommittal, but Hazel noticed the slight softening of her features—a wall coming down, stitch by delicate stitch.

"Absolutely," Hazel affirmed, her voice as comforting as the feel of merino wool slipping through one's fingers. "There's a certain magic in watching a single strand transform into something extraordinary. And the people—you'd be surprised how diverse the knitting circle is. It brings together folks from all walks of life, united by a common thread."

The older woman offered a nod, the corners of her mouth turning upward ever so slightly. She barely could look at Hazel, but that didn't mean much, because Hazel didn't see her wear any headphones throughout the flight.

Hazel leaned forward slightly, her enthusiasm undiminished by the older woman's polite disinterest. "I'm actually on my way to a fiber festival in Grenada," she said, her eyes lighting up at the thought. "It's a gathering of vendors with all sorts of fibers—wool, alpaca, silk, you name it. People come from all around to shop for materials to spin their own yarns." She glanced down at her pattern, tracing a line with her fingertip. "Each type of fiber has its own unique properties, leading to different results. The colors, the textures, the possibilities are endless."

The woman's response was a nonchalant nod, her attention shifting back to the phone on her lap as if it held greater allure than the vibrant tapestry Hazel painted with her words.

"Sounds… uh, interesting," the woman murmured, a cursory politeness lacing her tone, a fake smile across her face. "But I think I'll get back to my reading now." Rather than opening an e-book or news article, she propped the phone against the tray table and tapped away at a colorful game, rows of digital gems gleaming brightly on the screen.

With a soft sigh, Hazel turned back to her notebook, the pencil once again dancing in her hand as she plotted the next row of her cable knit design. It was a pattern only a fellow crafter could truly appreciate, much like the intricate game strategies lost on those who did not care to play.

Hazel's gaze drifted back to her notebook, the grid of squares awaiting transformation under her deft touch. Her fingers itched for the feel of yarn and needles, but for now, the pencil was her tool, sketching out a future cozy sweater or perhaps a snug beanie. With each symbol she penciled in, a mental image of the finished work blossomed, the tactile pleasure of creating something tangible from mere strands a source of constant wonder.

She let her thoughts weave through the memories of evenings spent on her couch, a half-finished scarf draped over her lap as she indulged in the latest melodrama on TV. The reality shows were a guilty pleasure, their outlandish antics a stark contrast to the soothing rhythm of her knitting. It was a dance of productivity and procrastination, where stitches formed in time with histrionic confessions and plot twists.

A chuckle bubbled up as she mused over the parallels between her craft and the woman's electronic diversion. Were they not both finding joy in simple repetition, one with threads of yarn, the other with pixels on a screen? Hazel's amusement was a private affair, contained within the bubble of her own contentment.

As the plane hummed along, anticipation curled within her like a skein of hand-dyed wool, vibrant and eager to unravel. The fiber festival beckoned, a promised land of fellow enthusiasts, each with their own tales of purls and patterns. She could almost hear the chatter of voices sharing tips, the laughter mingling with the clack of needles.

Her heart quickened at the thought of aisles brimming with raw materials, the air redolent with the earthy scent of wool and the tang of dyes. There, her language would be the common tongue, her knowledge an open book for others to leaf through and add to their own repositories of experience.

Everything about this trip was going to be perfect. The notion of perfection was subjective, of course, a patchwork quilt of expectations and serendipity. But for Hazel Stitchworth, knitter and sleuth, the promise of community, of shared passion, was all the perfection she sought.

And as the miles disappeared beneath the aircraft, carrying her closer to the heart of her world, Hazel's spirit soared, stitched wing by wing to the dream of what awaited her upon landing.

CHAPTER FOUR

Hazel stood outside the grand entrance of the conference center, her gaze tracing the ornate letters that crowned the doors like a promise of adventure. The annual fiber festival was an event she looked forward to all year, a vibrant tapestry woven into her calendar. She let out a long breath, one filled with the tension of cramped airplane seats and the faint hum of jet engines, now fading memories as her anticipation bubbled to the surface. She was ready to unravel some fun.

She shouldered her way through the bustle of the entrance, where the air buzzed with excitement palpable enough to knit with. A long table caught her eye, manned by volunteers with smiles almost as bright as the lanyards they handed out. Hazel sidled up to the table, her eyes sparkling with the eagerness of a child in a candy store.

"Name's Hazel Stitchworth," she announced, her voice threading through the chatter around her. The volunteer—a woman with hair the color of spun silver—flashed a grin and rifled through the badges.

"Ah, here we are," the volunteer said, presenting Hazel with a name badge emblazoned with her name in looping script. "Welcome, Hazel."

"Thank you!" Hazel replied, her fingers dancing with the lanyard before it settled around her neck, its weight a familiar comfort. It felt like donning armor, except instead of preparing for battle, she was gearing up for a quest for the softest wool and the most elusive of alpaca blends.

Badge secure, Hazel stepped over the threshold and into the heart of the festival. Her senses immediately flooded with the rich tapestry of the fiber world unfolding before her. She knew there'd be endless vendors to explore and mysteries to unwind, but for now, she allowed herself to simply be present in the whirlwind of creativity and camaraderie.

Hazel's gaze swept over the panorama of the fiber festival, a kaleidoscope of colors and textures that seemed to have leapt from the pages of a knitter's fairy tale. Booths unfurled before her like petals in a blooming garden, each one offering a vibrant feast for the senses. Skeins of yarn in every hue imaginable cascaded from tables and displays, begging to be touched. The air was thick with the scent of natural dyes, an intoxicating aroma that reminded her of earthy spices and sun-warmed wool.

She watched as vendors animatedly demonstrated the art of their craft, fingers nimbly carding fleece or drawing thread through a spindle's whirl. They showed off their exclusive fibers and pointed at presentations about their farms and the animals that made it possible.

It was like watching alchemists at work, spinning straw into gold. A tapestry of sounds filled the space: the soft shush of fibers being caressed, the rhythmic clicking of knitting needles, and the hum of excited chatter from fellow attendees all combined into a symphony of creativity.

The entire scene was Hazel's fantasy world made manifest, a place where the ordinary act of knitting was elevated to something magical. She felt a grin stretch across her face, her heart beating a little faster with the joy of it all.

"Excuse me," she murmured, stepping carefully around a cluster of onlookers who were engrossed in the intricacies of lacework. Her keen eyes roved over the booths, instinctively cataloging potential finds and noting techniques she might incorporate into her own shop.

Then, something familiar caught her eye: a sign that bore the silhouette of an Angora goat and the words "Mohair Marvels." Intrigued, Hazel weaved her way toward the booth, her ears perking up as she drew closer to the vendor's lilting voice.

"...and when blended with silk, it takes on this incredible luster," the booth owner was saying, lifting a skein that shimmered under the exhibit hall lights. "But it's not just about beauty; Mohair has strength. It's easy to spin, durable, and holds dye like a dream."

"Sounds almost too good to be true," Hazel quipped, a playful twinkle in her eye. She reached out, allowing the softness of the Mohair to roll between her fingers. It was like touching clouds, if clouds could be spun into yarn.

"Ah, but that's the magic of it," the vendor replied with a knowing smile. "One touch, and you're under its spell."

"Consider me thoroughly enchanted," Hazel said, her expression one of mock-seriousness. There was no denying the allure of the material; it was yet another marvel in a day that promised many. She tucked a strand of hair behind her ear and added, "I'll have to see how it fares with my needles. They can be quite discerning."

The booth owner chuckled, the sound warm and genuine. "I have no doubt they'll approve," she said. "Mohair is a knitter's best friend."

"Then I suppose introductions are in order," Hazel mused, her eyes dancing with delight. "I'm Hazel. I'd love a business card." The owner handed her a black and gray striped business card with 'Mohair Marvels' in large letters along with the owner's name, Tyson Higgins.

"Thanks, Tyson, I look forward to talking with you more later," Hazel told him before turning away.

With that, she mentally added Mohair to her ever-expanding list of must-haves, already envisioning the projects she would conjure with such a tantalizing textile. The festival was living up to every expectation, and then some.

Hazel's hand came to rest gently on the woman's shoulder, her voice a conspiratorial whisper. "You can't possibly need more Mohair after that haul last year." The woman turned, surprise etched across her features before recognition sparked in her eyes.

"Georgia!" Hazel exclaimed as her friend's expression shifted from shock to sheer delight.

"Hazel!" Georgia extended her arms, and in an instant, they were wrapped in an embrace that spoke volumes of the months spent apart. The hug was warm and tight, the kind that rekindles the heart's fond memories.

Pulling back just enough to see her friend's face, Hazel said with a smile, "I've missed you terribly. I'm so glad you're here again."

"Missed it? Not for the world!" Georgia replied, her Southern twang wrapping around each word like a cozy shawl. "And guess what? Leonard's supposed to be here too."

"Leonard?" Hazel's eyebrows rose, a smile tugging at the corners of her lips. Memories of last year's festival fluttered in her mind—the laughter, the shared admiration for exquisitely rare fibers, and the trio's unexpected kinship. "That would be fantastic!"

"Right?" Georgia's grin matched Hazel's enthusiasm. "He's just as eager to dive into the alpaca goldmine."

"Then we must find him," Hazel announced, sweeping a hand through the air as if to part the sea of fiber aficionados. "Think of it, the three of us weaving through this tapestry of color and texture—"

"Before the workshops start," Georgia finished for her, nodding vigorously. "We gotta soak in all this beauty while we can."

The two friends exchanged knowing glances, their shared anticipation for the day ahead as palpable as the vibrant skeins surrounding them. With a final squeeze of hands, they stepped forward together, ready to unravel the wonders of the fiber festival.

"Absolutely, let's track him down," Georgia agreed, her voice lilting with the excitement of the hunt. They set off, their steps in sync as they navigated through the labyrinth of yarn enthusiasts and kaleidoscopic stalls.

Hazel's gaze danced over the booths, each one a siren call with its array of fibers begging to be touched and transformed into something magical. She mentally bookmarked several stands with particularly plush merinos and vibrant silks, her fingers itching to loop and purl. But there would be time for that later; now was for reuniting.

"Ah, there he is!" Hazel exclaimed softly, spotting Leonard's unmistakable silhouette. His hair, normally a wild nest of curls, had been shorn to a bristly fuzz that made his ears stick out more than usual. She nudged Georgia, pointing discreetly at their friend who seemed engrossed in conversation.

Approaching, Hazel's stride slowed, her knitter's eyes picking up the finer details of the scene before her. Beside Leonard stood a figure tall and willowy, like a spindle from one of her more sophisticated knitting machines. Vivian Kensington towered on stilettos that Hazel reckoned could double as lethal weapons or makeshift knitting needles in a pinch.

Vivian turned her head, her smirk slicing through the warm atmosphere of the festival. It was the kind of look that could curdle fresh dye, and it took all of Hazel's resolve to not let her smile unravel completely.

"Vivian," Hazel greeted, her tone carefully neutral as she mustered a grin that felt more stitched together than any of her knitted creations. "Fancy seeing you here."

The air seemed to thicken with unspun wool, the tension palpable enough to felt. Georgia shifted beside her, a silent ally in the face of their common thread of frustration. The warmth of the festival dimmed ever so slightly under Vivian's cool shadow, but Hazel wouldn't let it snuff out the joy of the day. Not when there was so much yarn to be spun, both literally and figuratively.

Hazel let her gaze drift from the garish spectacle of Vivian's shoes up to the woman's face, where a triumphant glint matched the smirk tugging at the corner of her lips. "Oh, nice of you to join us," Vivian said in a tone that implied anything but.

"Actually, I've been enjoying the festival for the past hour," Hazel replied with an airy wave of her hand, as if batting away any insinuation of lateness. "There's plenty of time to look through all of the vendors and find some nice fibers."

Vivian tossed her hair, a cascade of sleek strands that seemed to mock the tangled skeins of yarn strewn about the booths. "Well," she drawled, "I suppose I forgot that not everyone has secured the best in the world. I've found an alpaca farmer who will be supplying me exclusively. So really, I don't need to source much here. Just showing my face to the vendors, letting them know I'm serious about business." Her voice carried the hint of superiority that came as naturally to her as purling did to Hazel.

"Isn't that fortunate for you," Hazel managed, her smile tight as a knit stitch on size zero needles. She didn't doubt for a second that Vivian had snagged herself a top-notch supplier; she was always weaving her way into the best deals. "I'll look forward to seeing this fabulous yarn of yours. Maybe I'll even get a chance to feel it."

"Perhaps," Vivian conceded, her nod curt, a business-like bob. "But I should be off. More to see and connections to make." And with that, she pivoted on those needle-sharp heels and strode off, each step a pronounced click against the floor, like the tap of bamboo knitting needles in the hands of a speed knitter.

Hazel watched her go, the back of Vivian's designer blazer retreating into the distance—a sharp contrast to the vibrant and homey hues of the yarns surrounding them. Shaking her head slightly, Hazel turned to Georgia with a wry smile. "Shall we dive back into this woolly wonderland?" she quipped, ready to unravel the tension Vivian left in her wake with a good dose of fiber fondling and friend time.

Leonard's expression was a comical mix of relief and bemusement as Vivian Kensington's retreating figure finally blended into the colorful tapestry of the festival crowd. "Thank you, Hazel," he exhaled heavily, as if he'd been holding his breath for far too long. "I thought she'd never leave. She practically had me pinned against the alpaca display with her success stories."

Hazel let out a sigh, her fingers idly playing with the edge of her lanyard, the name badge bobbing gently against her chest. "If only Vivian didn't always have to knit herself a pedestal to stand on," she mused aloud. "She's got the skills, no doubt, but that attitude... It just unravels any chance of a real partnership in this business."

Georgia nodded empathetically, her own badge swaying in agreement. "It's like she's knitting with silk thread on bamboo needles—smooth with the vendors but rough with everyone else. I get exhausted just trying to stitch together a conversation with her that doesn't end in knots." She glanced at the surrounding booths, each a burst of color and creativity—a stark contrast to Vivian's steely demeanor.

"Work with her?" Hazel shook her head, her curls bouncing slightly. "No way. I'd rather try to cable without a needle." Her voice carried a hint of jest, but her eyes were serious, reflecting the conviction behind her words.

Leonard adjusted his glasses, peering eagerly at the labyrinth of booths before them. "Well, I'm here to see some fibers," he announced with a hint of excitement in his voice, "and we've only got a few hours before that seminar by Eduardo Valdez starts. You know, the alpaca farmer?"

"Absolutely," Hazel replied, her eyes lighting up at the mention of Eduardo's name. She brushed a loose strand of hair behind her ear and smiled. "I have to get my supply from him, just like every year. It'll be nice to hear him speak again." Her fingers instinctively found the soft wool of her scarf, a tactile reminder of last year's prized find.

Georgia, ever the motivator, clapped her hands together. "Then we should get going," she chimed in, her eyes sparkling with the same anticipation they all shared for the wonders tucked within the festival's fold. "There's lots to see."

And with that, the three friends melded into the parade of yarn and fiber enthusiasts that filled the aisles. The air buzzed with conversations about plying techniques and dye lots, while the scent of freshly spun wool mingled with the subtle fragrance of natural dyes. They passed by a booth festooned with skeins of hand-dyed yarn, each hue more vibrant than the last, beckoning with whispers of potential projects.

"Look at those colors," Hazel murmured, almost to herself, her gaze briefly ensnared by the dance of shades and tones. But Georgia gently tugged at her elbow, steering her forward, and Leonard pointed past a bustling crowd gathered around a demonstration on spindle spinning.

"Come on," he said, with a twinkle in his eye that told of his eagerness to explore, "the good stuff is this way."

As they wove through the throng, Hazel couldn't help but let out a soft chuckle—here they were, a trio of kindred spirits, united by their love for the craft and the chase of the perfect fiber. It was moments like these that stitched their friendship tighter, a tapestry of shared joy in a world woven from the very threads they adored.

CHAPTER FIVE

Hazel shifted in the hotel's stiff chair, her legs itching to spring up and pace. Beside her, Georgia was a picture of composure, while Leonard had the fidgets, his leg bouncing like a jackhammer with anticipation.

"Isn't this just thrilling?" Leonard's whisper cut through the hum of eager chatter around them. "Eduardo always knows how to spin a good yarn about alpaca farming."

She was about to chime in with her agreement when the room hushed as if someone had turned down the volume on a giant remote control. Eduardo had taken the stage, an unassuming figure who could easily be mistaken for just another enthusiast, yet to Hazel, he was the maestro of merino, the sultan of softness.

"Good afternoon, everyone," Eduardo began, his voice soothing yet authoritative, like a warm scarf wrapped around your shoulders. "Can everyone hear me okay at the back?"

Hazel couldn't help but smile. This man knew his audience as well as his alpacas. He wasn't just a farmer; he was an artisan, and every fiber he produced was a testament to his craft.

"Today, I brought along some samples of our finest alpaca fleece." Eduardo's excitement was palpable as his assistants began passing around small tufts of fleece. It was like watching a relay race of fluffy clouds being handed from one set of eager hands to another.

As each participant fondled the fleece, nodding appreciatively or murmuring to their neighbor, Hazel leaned back, arms crossed. She knew these samples would be exceptional; after all, she sourced most of her shop's premier fibers from Eduardo's farm. It was a partnership woven from mutual respect and the shared love of a good knit—or purl, depending on the day.

Watching the fleece make its rounds, she envisioned the myriad of projects they could inspire. Scarves that felt like a kitten's whisper against the skin, beanies as cozy as a hug from an old friend, and mittens that could make even the chilliest mornings seem inviting.

"Feel the difference in textures," Eduardo was saying, his voice a melody over the heads of the attendees. "Each has its unique quality and purpose."

Hazel caught a glimpse of the man himself, his hands animated as though each finger were conducting an invisible orchestra of threads and fibers. There was no denying it—Eduardo was in his element, and she wouldn't have missed this seminar for the world.

The plush samples finally made their way to Hazel's expectant hands. She took a moment to close her eyes, letting her fingers dance over the fibers as if they were keys on a piano, each note striking a chord of softness and warmth. The baby alpaca fleece was lighter than air, a testament to its high quality, while the suri alpaca boasted a luster that rivaled the sheen of silk.

"Notice the micron count here," Eduardo's voice carried through the room, rich with enthusiasm. "It determines the softness of the fiber. Lower means softer, and ideal for next-to-skin wear."

Hazel nodded along, her tactile senses in agreement with his expert commentary. The difference was palpable, like comparing the whisper of a gentle breeze to the smooth touch of still water.

But as Eduardo continued, detailing the intricate process of turning these heavenly tufts into yarn, Hazel's mind wandered just a stitch away from the present. She needed to stock up on merino wool, and perhaps it was time to explore the delicate world of cashmere. Eduardo's seminar had sparked a new level of curiosity—she could already imagine the luxurious skeins nestled amongst her shop's shelves.

"Any questions so far?" Eduardo's voice snapped Hazel back to the conference room.

"Um, no," she murmured, shaking her head slightly as if to dislodge her wandering thoughts. "Just thinking about my next purchases."

Her gaze lingered on the speaker, admiring his passion as he described sustainable grazing practices. It wasn't just his knowledge that captivated her; it was the fervor with which he shared it, every word painting a vivid tapestry of life on his farm.

Eduardo's hands moved with the same precision and care that Hazel applied to her knitting needles. It was then she realized that whether it was unraveling a mystery or entwining strands of yarn, it was all about piecing together the perfect pattern. And right now, the pattern was telling her to listen closely—not just to Eduardo's seminar, but to the subtle hints that might lead her to the finest cashmere vendor at the festival. Her fingers itched to knit the threads of this new quest into something tangible.

***

The seminar had wrapped up in a flurry of applause, and the conference room buzzed with excitement. Everyone was locked onto Eduardo throughout the entire presentation, or maybe that was just Hazel. She thought it was the best seminar the festival had to date. And that definitely had nothing to do with the fact that she was a long time buyer and friend of Eduardo.

She rose from her seat, stretching her legs as she made her way to the front of the room. The throng of attendees seemed to part for her, or perhaps it was just her determined stride that cleared the path. She spotted Eduardo engaged in an animated conversation with a couple of festival-goers, his hands gesticulating as he shared one last tidbit of alpaca wisdom.

Catching sight of Hazel, his face lit up, and he excused himself, stepping away to greet her with a warmth that matched the softness of his prized fleece. "Hazel! I'm so glad you could make it," he said, his voice genuine.

"Miss your seminar? I wouldn't dream of it," Hazel replied with a grin, "You're my favorite supplier, and I wouldn't get my alpacas' bounty from anyone else."

Eduardo chuckled, rubbing the back of his neck modestly. "And how are you finding the festival? Enjoying the cornucopia of fibers?"

"Let's be real, Eduardo, I'm mostly here for the alpaca action. But yes, there are some nice booths," Hazel teased, her eyes twinkling. "Actually, on that note, I wanted to ask if you know any good cashmere suppliers? I know goats aren't really your field."

He nodded, understanding the unspoken respect between different areas of expertise. "I might have someone in mind for you," he said, a knowing smile playing on his lips. Their laughter mingled and lingered in the air, a comfortable melody amidst the residual chatter of the departing crowd.

"Absolutely, Hazel," Eduardo enthused, his eyes twinkling with the kind of sincerity that comes from a genuine love for his trade. "Paula is your go-to for cashmere. Her goats are pampered more than most house pets, and you can feel it in every fiber."

Hazel sighed in relief, her shoulders visibly relaxing. The thought of navigating the labyrinth of vendors without guidance was like trying to find a dropped stitch in a complex cable pattern. "Thank heavens," she said, tucking a stray flyer back into her tote bag crammed with colorful pamphlets boasting 'top-notch quality.' With a conspiratorial lean, she nudged Eduardo's elbow. "But we can't all be the best, now can we?"

His laughter was a low rumble, and he shook his head, leaning in so only Hazel could hear. "It's just us here, Hazel. I'm glad it's not too lonely at the top. Speaking of, I have something I want to tell you by the end of the festival."

"Oh? A secret of some kind?" Hazel asked, a smirk growing across her face.

"It's going to come out and I don't want you to worry about our business together," he replied matter-of-factly.

Hazel's smirk faded. "Everything okay?"

"Yes, yes. It's just some news, it's about me. I can't talk about it yet, but remember to stop by before you leave the festival? I'd like to tell you in person."

She couldn't tell if Eduardo was happy or sad about the news he had to share. So she couldn't even guess what he would have to say to her. But the fact that he said it wasn't going to impact their businesses was enough to comfort her through the rest of the festival.

"Of course I will," she said with a smile.

Hazel turned slightly to see that a queue had formed behind her, a line of eager attendees waiting to soak up Eduardo's expertise on alpaca farming.

"Goodness, look at this crowd," Hazel remarked, stepping aside. "Before I get trampled by the wool enthusiasts, where should I meet you for our usual handoff?"

"Come to the farm tomorrow," Eduardo suggested with an easy smile, thumbing toward the door as if pointing the way. "You can meet the alpacas, see where the magic happens. I'll make sure you leave with the cream of the crop."

Hazel's heart did a little purl stitch of joy. "I'd be honored, Eduardo. I've never been before. It would be so thrilling to see."

They exchanged a final smile, one that held the warmth of long-standing partnership and mutual respect. As Hazel stepped away, allowing the next person to bask in Eduardo's genial presence, she already envisioned the sun-dappled fields of his farm, the hum of contented alpacas, and the promise of yarn yet to be spun.

Hazel weaved through the dispersing crowd, her mind still looping Eduardo's words like a well-practiced cable stitch. She spotted Georgia and Leonard engaged in an animated conversation near a poster of an alpaca that looked as though it was smirking at the attendees.

"Hey, you two, how about we hunt down some dinner? I'm famished," Hazel quipped as she approached them, hoping to entice her friends with the prospect of a shared meal.

Georgia shook her head, her forehead creasing with concern. "Oh, Hazel, I'd love to, but there's a snarl in my inventory count back at the store. I've got to straighten it out before it becomes a real tangled mess."

"Surely it can wait?" Hazel suggested, although she knew Georgia's dedication to her business was as tightly wound as the yarn on a spindle.

"Sorry, dear, it's like dropped stitches in a complex pattern; better to address them right away," Georgia said, already fishing her phone from her purse.

Leonard offered an apologetic smile. "And I have reservations at Chez Laine. It's this fancy place downtown, and my assistant's been dying to try it. Can't stand her up."

"Guess it's just me and my lonesome stomach then," Hazel said with a playful sigh. "Perhaps the hotel restaurant will have a cozy corner for one."

"Next time, Hazel. Enjoy your meal," Leonard said, patting her shoulder as he turned away, his assistant's name probably already ringing in his ears.

"Good luck with the numbers, Georgia," Hazel called out as her friend hurried off with the phone pressed to her ear.

"Thanks, hon. Let's catch up tomorrow!" Georgia's voice trailed off into the hubbub of the conference center.

With her dining options dwindling faster than yarn at a clearance sale, Hazel pulled out her phone, tapping the screen to bring up the hotel map. The digital layout sprawled across her screen like a labyrinth designed by a particularly mischievous knitter. The Mediterranean place sounded promising, tucked away beyond a maze of conference rooms and corridors.

"Okay, Stitchworth, let's chart the quickest course to sustenance," Hazel muttered to herself, squinting at the tiny icons. She followed the map's dotted line with a finger, imagining the tang of olives and the sizzle of grilled meat awaiting her. With a newfound determination, she set off, her hunger driving her forward like the promise of a new knitting project. Her footsteps echoed lightly on the polished floor, marking her solo venture through the echoing halls toward the promise of a feast fit for a queen—or at least a very hungry yarn shop owner.

CHAPTER SIX

Hazel stood in line at the hotel's Mediterranean restaurant, absently twisting a stray yarn around her finger as she contemplated the menu overhead. The place was a curious blend of casual and chic, with brushed metal fixtures casting a soft glow over the colorful mosaic tiles that lined the walls. It was the ‘grab-and-go’ sort of establishment within the grandiose hotel, but it didn't skimp on ambiance or array of choices.

She stepped up to the counter when her turn arrived, greeted by the warm smile of the attendant. "I'll have the chicken kabobs and a side of Greek salad, please," she said, her gaze lingering on the vibrant greens and ripe tomatoes behind the glass display.

"Coming right up!" chirped the server as Hazel handed over her card, the transaction punctuating her order with a beep.

As she turned, ready to sidestep to the pick-up area, her shoulder met an unexpected obstacle—a solid form that grunted softly upon impact. "Oh! I'm so sorry," Hazel exclaimed, her hands fluttering like the wings of a distressed sparrow.

The obstacle turned out to be a man, not just any man, but one who could have easily stepped out of a travel brochure for Greece itself—tall, with an olive complexion that testified his familiarity with sunny climes. He straightened, and Hazel took in the chiseled jawline and deep-set eyes that seemed to capture the warmth of the Mediterranean Sea.

"No harm done," he assured her in a voice smooth as aged whiskey. With a practiced ease, he retrieved a takeout box from the countertop, his movements confident and sure.

"Well, good," Hazel managed to reply, her cheeks warming faster than yarn in the sun. The man offered her a curt nod before turning to leave, his departure leaving Hazel briefly adrift in a sea of admiration. She couldn't help but note the effortless grace with which he moved, as if the world were his to traverse without a single snag.

With a shake of her head, Hazel tried to untangle her thoughts, returning her focus to the anticipation of a savory meal. But as she waited for her name to be called, those deep-sea eyes lingered in her mind, stirring more curiosity than anything else.

"Excuse me," a voice called from behind Hazel, halting her mid-thought.

She turned, almost instinctively, to find the man she'd just run into smiling at her, his eyes twinkling with an amiable light. The simple gesture smoothed out the creases of hesitation on her face, replacing them with a tentative smile.

"I was planning to dine solo in my room," he began, his hand casually brushing against the takeout box as if to emphasize his solitary plans. "But I couldn't help but notice you're alone too. Were you planning on doing something?"

The invitation hung in the air like an unexpected pattern alteration that Hazel hadn't predicted but found herself eager to explore. She shook her head gently, the curls of her hair bouncing slightly, as she replied, "No, no one's joining me. I was just going to head up to my room, too."

"Then maybe we could keep each other company?" His suggestion came as smoothly as silk yarn slipping through the needles, and Hazel felt the corners of her mouth lift into a genuine smile.

"Company would be lovely," Hazel responded, feeling flattered and intrigued by this unexpected turn in her evening.

"Excellent," he said, his grin broadening. "I'll secure us a spot."

As if on cue, the bustling atmosphere of the restaurant was pierced by the sharp call of "Hazel!" from the counter. She excused herself with, "That's me; just let me grab my food. Maybe find us a table?"

He nodded, his expression an intricate blend of charm and politeness, and she made her way to collect her order.

With her tray laden with the fragrant kabobs and a crisp Greek salad, Hazel scanned the dining area. She spotted him in a cozy corner, his form a silent invitation against the backdrop of chatter and clinking cutlery. Approaching the table, she took in how he examined his dish with an almost childlike curiosity—an endearing sight.

"Looks good, doesn't it?" she remarked, setting down her tray and taking a seat across from him.

"Indeed," he agreed, looking up from his plate, his attention shifting seamlessly from his meal to her. "Some flavors are worth unraveling, much like a well-spun yarn."

Hazel laughed softly, appreciating the attempt at knitting lingo. "Exactly. Though I'm hoping there are no knots in this particular yarn," she quipped, gesturing towards her meal with a playful raise of her eyebrow.

Their conversation knitted together as easily as Hazel's practiced fingers would have woven yarn, and as they settled into the meal, the sense of warmth between them grew, slowly.

Hazel eased into the chair, the warmth from the freshly prepared kabobs rising to greet her as she settled. Across from her, the man extended a friendly hand, his smile unwavering.

"Name's Liam, Liam Blackwell," he introduced himself with an ease that seemed to reflect his comfortable demeanor.

"Nice to meet you, Liam," Hazel said, but before she could return the introduction, he interjected with a knowing tilt of his head.

"Hazel, right? They called out your name up there." His gesture aimed toward the counter where she had ordered just moments ago.

"Yes, that's me—Hazel Stitchworth." She nodded, a strand of hair falling forward which she quickly tucked behind her ear. She speared a piece of tender kabob, bringing it to her lips, her palate greeting the burst of savory herbs and spices.

"Are you here for the fiber festival?" Liam inquired, his eyes holding a spark of genuine curiosity.

With a mouthful of Greek salad, Hazel gave an affirmative nod, then swallowed before responding. "Mhm, are you?" she asked, trying not to sound too surprised that someone like him would attend such an event.

"Absolutely," Liam said, taking a sip of water and setting the glass down with a soft clink against the table. There was a gleam of enthusiasm in his eyes that caught the restaurant's ambient lighting. "I've always been intrigued by the industry—the idea of handspun yarn, the textures, the processes that go into creating something so unique."

Hazel raised her eyebrows in pleasant surprise, her fork pausing mid-air. It wasn't every day she met someone who shared her passion for the craft, especially at a hotel's fast-casual dining spot. "Yeah, exactly," she agreed, resuming her meal. "I actually run my own store, Knitter's Nook. It's filled with all sorts of hand-spun yarn and knitting paraphernalia."

"Knitter's Nook? That's a sweet name," Liam remarked, a note of respect threading through his words. "Your reputation for quality must precede you."

Hazel felt a blush rise to her cheeks, flattered by the recognition. "Well, we try our best," she said modestly, tucking into her food once more. Her taste buds danced to the zesty notes of olive oil and feta cheese mingling on her tongue, a culinary prelude to what was shaping up to be an unexpectedly delightful evening.

Hazel's fork was halfway to her mouth, laden with a perfectly proportioned bite of Greek salad, when the rising cadence of a heated discussion snagged her attention. She turned her head ever so slightly, eyes landing on the source—a table where Eduardo and his son Carlos were ensconced in what appeared to be a family feud. Eduardo's hands were animated, punctuating the air like exclamation points, while Carlos seemed to recoil with each verbal jab.

Hazel remembered all of the times that Eduardo came with his children, both his son and daughter. Of course lately it was always only his son. She didn't know much about them, because they usually talked only about business or personal lives, not his family. She just knew that he had kids, and he loved them, but no details. Something about the sight in front of her gnawed at her—a detail out of place. Carlos had been notably absent from Eduardo's seminar earlier that day, an oddity for a duo usually seen side by side at such events.

Her focus on the unfolding drama caused her hand to betray her, and she watched, almost in slow motion, as a cherry tomato made a bid for freedom, slipping from her fork and performing a graceful dive back into the bowl. The splatter was minimal, but enough to jerk Hazel back to her own table, where Liam's expectant gaze held a hint of concern—or was it curiosity?

"Sorry," Hazel said, offering him an apologetic tilt of the head as she set her fork down. "Can you repeat that?"

"Sure," Liam replied, his voice smooth as he leaned back just a fraction, a gesture inviting her to relax. "I was asking if you'd had the chance to see the gardens yet. They're quite a sight during the day, but I've heard they're even more stunning at night with all the lights."

"Ah." Hazel shook her head lightly, her chestnut curls bouncing with the motion. "No, I've been tangled up with work for most of my stay here. It seems my yarns have knitted themselves into a rather demanding schedule."

"Understandable," Liam said with an easy smile, reaching for his glass of water. "The life of a dedicated craftswoman is rarely a leisurely one."

"Indeed," Hazel agreed, skewering a piece of lettuce with renewed determination. "But I suppose one must occasionally unravel their commitments to appreciate the beauty around them."

"Exactly," Liam nodded, his eyes alight with a shared understanding. "Sometimes, you just need to drop a stitch or two to make room for the unexpected pleasures of life."

"Or the unexpected company," Hazel added, her gaze meeting his with an unspoken acknowledgment of the pleasant twist their evening had taken.

Liam's suggestion hung in the air like a delicate thread, poised to unravel or weave into something more. He watched her reaction with anticipation, his eyes widening slightly as if he'd just pulled on a loose end without meaning to. "Of course," he backpedaled gently, slouching ever so slightly in his chair, a self-conscious grin tugging at the corner of his mouth, "you don't have to. We've only just met, and I wouldn't want you to feel as though you need to follow me around all evening...but I thought, it could be fun."

Hazel couldn't help but smile at Liam's eagerness, which seemed to have caught even him by surprise. The warmth in her chest bloomed like wool soaking up dye, spreading a soft hue of amusement throughout her. "After dinner would be lovely," she said, her tone light and playful. "I'd enjoy seeing the gardens with you."

Relief washed over Liam's features, smoothing out the creases of his wide-eyed moment. His smile brightened, sincere and infectious. "Well good," he replied, leaning forward with renewed enthusiasm. "It's settled then. They say it's the best time to visit, and I'm certain it will be even better with a bit of company."

"Company is always good," Hazel agreed, her own smile lingering like the afterglow of sunset. As they continued their meal, the lighthearted banter flowed between them as easily as yarn through expert fingers. She found herself savoring each bite of her kabobs and Greek salad, the flavors mingling pleasantly with the unfolding conversation.

Glancing across the table at Liam, Hazel realized she was genuinely enjoying this unexpected encounter. There was something about his genuine interest in the fiber arts and his thoughtful observations that spun a comforting camaraderie. The prospect of strolling through the hotel's gardens later wasn't just an item on her itinerary; it was a shared adventure she found herself anticipating with a sense of excitement that surprised her.

"Who knew a simple bump at a Mediterranean restaurant would lead to an impromptu garden tour?" she mused inwardly, her mind already wandering to the textures and fragrances awaiting them beneath the evening lights. Yes, this might indeed turn out to be quite fun.

CHAPTER SEVEN

Hazel Stitchworth peered at her reflection in the hotel room mirror, a small frown creasing her brow as she unhooked the long dangly earrings that had felt so out of place dangling from her lobes. They clinked gently as she set them on the dresser, her hands then smoothing down her jeans with a satisfied nod. The cute blouse she had chosen draped comfortably over her frame, striking the perfect balance between casual and charming for her evening stroll with Liam in the gardens.

"Comfort over fashion," she murmured to herself, her lips curving into a wry smile. The corners of her mouth quirked up further as she considered the pun – her love for knitting often weaving its way into her daily thoughts.

She gave herself a final once-over and grabbed her purse, the soft leather familiar and reassuring under her touch. With one last approving glance at her ensemble in the mirror, Hazel walked with determined steps to the elevator, pressing the button and waiting for the soft ding that signaled its arrival. As the doors slid open, she stepped inside, descending towards what she hoped would be a pleasant and enlightening evening.

The gentle hum of the elevator was a momentary cocoon, and Hazel mulled over the curious blend of anticipation and trust bubbling within her. Trusting Liam, a man she barely knew, felt as daring as attempting a new, complicated knitting pattern without a guide. Yet, there was something about him – an earnestness, perhaps – that knit together a sense of security.

Maybe it's the way he talks about textiles, she pondered, her thoughts slipping their way through her mind. *Or how his eyes light up with history.*

As the elevator chimed its arrival at the lobby, the doors parted to reveal the grandeur that spread out before her. The space was expansive, a symphony of marbled floors and gilded accents that echoed with the soft murmur of guests and the subtle strains of a piano playing somewhere in the distance.

"Here goes nothing," Hazel whispered to herself, stepping out into the opulence with a newfound spring in her step.

Her gaze swept across the lobby, taking in the clusters of people chatting amiably or lounging in the plush seating areas. She could feel the buzz of conversation, the collective warmth of human presence – a comforting reminder that even in the company of a near-stranger, she wasn't entirely alone. It bolstered her confidence as she made her way towards the large front doors, her heels clicking lightly against the polished floor.

"Besides," she thought with a chuckle, "if he turns out to be a rogue, I've got my knitting needles. And I'm not afraid to use them."

Hazel's steps slowed as a cacophony of voices rose to greet her, the words "Save the animals!" and "No more cruelty" rippling through the air like wayward stitches in an otherwise peaceful tapestry. A group of protesters, their signs held high like banners at a medieval joust, were making their presence felt just to the left of the grand entrance.

"Curious," Hazel murmured, a frown knitting her brows together as she approached for a closer look. Each sign was a patchwork of passionate pleas, the colors vivid against the fading daylight.

"Animal friends not food!" one sign read, the letters bold and accusing. Hazel's eyes scanned the crowd, landing on a woman whose long brown hair cascaded over a yellow shirt emblazoned with a heart encircling an earthy paw print. The sign she wielded pointed a finger squarely at Eduardo, claiming his farms were less than up to par.

"Valdez hates his wool suppliers," it said.

Surely, they had it wrong. She knew Eduardo, a man whose love for his animals was woven into every aspect of his business. He spoke of them not as inventory, but as living beings under his care. Where had these people pulled such a crazy theory?

Hazel thought about how information could become muddled sometimes. Yet, she wasn't here to pick apart protests; the gardens, and Liam, awaited.

Shaking her head slightly, she turned away from the commotion, the chants becoming a distant hum as her focus shifted to the promise of an enchanting walk through greenery and blooms. A soft sigh escaped her lips – there would be time enough to follow this peculiar thread later. For now, the garden beckoned, and with it, stories of history and architecture that promised to be as rich and intricate as the most complex of knitting patterns.

Hazel's mind stitched back to a seminar she had attended, one where Eduardo was the speaker. She remembered how he had stood at the podium, his voice woven with conviction as he spoke about the welfare of his animals. His belief that they deserved comfort right up until the end was not just a part of his speech; it was embroidered into the fabric of his business model.

"Money is not the fleece I'm after," Eduardo had said, gesturing with hands calloused from work, not from counting cash. "It's the trust of these creatures, the assurance that we honor their contribution with respect and care."

Hazel hoped the protesters would unravel the truth about Eduardo themselves. After all, it wasn't her mystery to solve – at least, not tonight. With a last glance at the fervent crowd, she turned her attention away, letting the tension in her shoulders fall away like dropped stitches.

As she approached the hotel's grand entrance once more, Hazel caught sight of the gardens Liam had painted with words earlier that day. Her breath caught slightly at the view – it was a tapestry of nature meticulously laid out before her eyes. The shrubbery, flowers, and bushes were perfectly arranged, as though each had been positioned by an artist's hand. Small rounded lights peppered throughout the greenery cast a gentle glow that seemed to dance across the foliage, bringing the scene to life in the encroaching dusk.

"Wow," Hazel couldn't help but exhale the word, soft and full of wonder, as if speaking too loudly might disturb the serenity of the garden's tableau.

The delicate scent of blooming flowers mingled with the earthy aroma of the moist soil, creating a fragrance as inviting as freshly baked bread. The light chirp of crickets added a natural melody to the atmosphere, a quiet symphony for any who took the time to listen.

She stepped forward, her shoes whispering against the stone path that welcomed her into this verdant paradise. Each plant seemed to lean towards her, sharing its story in a language without words, and for a moment, Hazel felt as if she were a character in one of those romance novels she'd chuckle at in her shop, embarking on an adventure of her own.

"It's just like I said, isn't it?" Liam's voice was gentle but carried an unmistakable note of pride.

Startled from her reverie, Hazel turned to find him approaching, his attire a notch above casual with a crisply buttoned shirt that seemed to mirror the elegance of their surroundings. "Yes, it's gorgeous," she agreed, her eyes sparkling with appreciation. "I've never seen anything quite like it."

Liam's smile broadened as he gestured toward the carefully curated greenery. "The history of the garden is beautiful too. It was actually put here before they transformed this place into a hotel. All this," he swept his hand across the view, "was part of a mansion, created by a famous architect."

Hazel glanced back at the modern façade of the hotel, then at Liam with furrowed brows—a knit in her forehead matching the complexity of her yarn patterns. "There's no way that's true," she challenged playfully.

"Ah, but it is," Liam nodded, his eyes gleaming with the thrill of sharing a hidden tale. "They obviously did major renovations and expanded the property, but originally, it was a mansion. And the man who built it, he was doing it for his wife, who tragically only enjoyed it for a year before passing away."

"Really?" Hazel's skepticism gave way to a tender curiosity as she listened.

"Yes." He leaned closer, lowering his voice to a near-whisper as if confiding a secret. "The owner was so heartbroken that he poured his soul into creating this garden for her. He believed she could still live through the earth, through every blossom and blade of grass."

"That's...beautiful." A soft sigh escaped Hazel's lips. The sentiment resonated within her, much like the yarns she intertwined to create something timeless and comforting.

Without a second thought, she reached out and took Liam's arm, drawn by a mix of admiration and an unspoken connection. Together, they began to stroll down the stone pathway that meandered through the heart of the garden.

"Every step here feels like a stitch in time," Hazel mused, her fingers grazing the textured sleeve of Liam's shirt as if to memorize the moment through touch. "A seamless blend of past and present."

"Exactly," Liam replied, his voice rich with enthusiasm. "And every plant here has its own story, much like the fibers you're so fond of weaving into your creations."

As they walked, the shadows danced lightly around them, the lights casting a soft glow on their path. The world beyond the garden felt miles away, and Hazel couldn't help but think that perhaps this walk might just be the most enchanting thing she'd ever experienced. Like out of a storybook, she was walking through beautiful gardens with a handsome stranger.

The soft illumination from the rounded lights scattered throughout played with the shadows, adding an ethereal quality to the foliage around them.

"Since the original owner passed away," Liam shared, his voice taking on a reverent tone, "his estate was sold off. But when this hotel company took over, they had to agree to one important condition—the garden had to be preserved as is, except for the necessary maintenance to keep it alive."

Hazel looked around, her eyes wide with wonder at the uninterrupted splendor before her. "So, all of this," she gestured broadly, "is essentially how it was all those years ago? Untouched?"

"Exactly," Liam confirmed, pride in his voice. "They were allowed to add things like the lighting we see, but nothing living can be cut down unless it's already dead. What you're seeing now is very much what he built for her."

"Remarkable," Hazel breathed out, her heart swelling with the romance of it all. "That story might just be more beautiful than the garden itself."

Liam chuckled softly, the sound mixing harmoniously with the evening chorus of crickets. "I thought you might appreciate it. I did some digging into the history before I came here. It's captivated me ever since."

Curiosity piqued, Hazel tilted her head, her soft curls brushing against his arm. "But how did you unearth such a tale? Surely, a place like this would prefer to tout its luxury over its legacy."

"Ah, but that's where you're wrong," Liam said with a twinkle in his eye. "I'm quite the history aficionado. Uncovering stories like this one is what I live for."

Hazel's lips quirked up in an amused smile as they strolled past a bed of vibrant flowers. There was something infectious about Liam's passion for the past—a kindred spirit, yet his threads were woven with historical facts rather than yarn. She pondered for a moment, realizing the parallel between them; both sought to preserve and cherish the beauty of bygone times. He with his stories, and she with her stitches.

"Seems like you have a knack for finding the fabric of history," Hazel mused, the pun hanging between them like an offering.

"Let's just say, if history were a tapestry, I'd be eager to trace every thread. I do work as a historian and I've always been a huge history buff," Liam replied, clearly enjoying the metaphorical exchange.

Their laughter blended seamlessly with the symphony of the night, and as they walked, Hazel felt a warm glow that had little to do with the surrounding lights. Here, in this lush sanctuary, with a man who shared her appreciation for the delicate patterns of the past, she sensed that this walk might just weave itself into the fabric of her fondest memories.

Liam's eyes glinted with the excitement of a secret as he leaned closer to Hazel. "You know, there's an entire chapter I've yet to share about this place," he said in a hushed tone that gave the words an air of conspiracy.

"Really?" Hazel perked up, her curiosity piqued like a pattern unraveling before her. "I would love to hear more," she said, her own voice lowering to match his conspiratorial whisper.

"Then prepare to be enchanted," Liam began, gesturing toward a secluded part of the garden where moonlight played on petals that seemed to shimmer with their own internal light. "There are flowers here that bloom but once a year. They say it's nature's way of teaching us to appreciate fleeting beauty."

Hazel watched as one of the blossoms quivered in the gentle night breeze, its delicate dance a quiet celebration of life's ephemeral moments. She was captivated, her senses fully engaged in this nocturnal world of wonders Liam was unveiling.

"Once a year, huh?" Hazel mused, her gaze lingering on the rare blooms. "It reminds me of certain yarns that come around just once in a season. You have to cherish them while you can." A smile touched her lips at the thought; she always did enjoy the parallel between her craft and the natural world.

"Exactly," Liam nodded, pleased by her understanding. "And just think, tomorrow you'll be exploring Eduardo's farm. Who knows what unique fibers you might discover there?"

"Or mysteries," Hazel added playfully, her sleuth's mind never quite at rest, even amidst such tranquility.

"Or mysteries," Liam echoed with a warm laugh, clearly appreciating her wit.

As they continued along the path, flanked by the silent sentinels of ancient shrubs and trees, Hazel couldn't help but think that this trip might indeed be her best one yet. With each step, she felt herself weaving into the tapestry of history and intrigue that this place—and Liam—had to offer.

CHAPTER EIGHT

Hazel Stitchworth maneuvered the car rental through the winding roads that ribboned across the Spanish countryside. The early morning sunlight spilled over the rolling hills, gilding them with a warm glow that seemed to set the world ablaze with soft gold. Rows upon rows of olive trees danced in the gentle breeze, their silvery leaves whispering secrets of the land as she passed by.

She couldn't help but marvel at the sheer vastness of the landscape. Here, properties were spread out like patchwork quilts, each a private kingdom unto itself, nestled between seemingly endless acres of farmland. It was a stark contrast to the coziness of Knotsville, where everyone knew each other's names and backstories as intricately as the patterns of their most treasured knitted blankets.

Eduardo's farm seemed to be miles away from the nearest neighbor. Or maybe Hazel just wasn't used to places like this, vast expanses of space with homes inbetween.

Hazel glanced at the GPS, which assured her she was almost there, just one more turn off the main road. She had been looking forward to seeing Eduardo's farm ever since he'd described it to her during their last video call—his voice weaving tales of alpacas grazing under the Spanish sun, their wool soon to become part of her boutique's exclusive collection.

As she neared the designated driveway, her train of thought derailed when an unexpected figure appeared in the middle of the road—an alpaca, standing as nonchalantly as if it were waiting for a bus rather than blocking a country lane.

"Of all the things..." Hazel laughed softly to herself, bemused. The sight was so incongruous yet delightful; it was like something out of a whimsical storybook. She slowed the car to a stop, not wanting to startle the animal. "Well, this is certainly a 'woolly' unique welcome committee."

The alpaca looked at her with mild curiosity, its long lashes giving it an air of innocence that belied its adventurous escape. Hazel couldn't help but smile at the creature, her heart lightened by the absurdity of the situation.

Hazel peered over the steering wheel, her gaze following a trail of errant alpacas dotting the road ahead. One ambled aimlessly, another nibbled at the verge of the road, and a third played hide-and-seek among the olive bushes—each one an escape artist in its own right. "Looks like Eduardo's got a breakout on his hands," she muttered, the puzzle of the situation igniting a spark of sleuthing delight in her.

Without hesitation, Hazel swung open the car door, the gentle hum of the engine falling silent as she cut the ignition. She stepped out onto the dusty country lane, her sneakers crunching softly on the gravel. The air was filled with the scent of wild thyme and rosemary, a fragrant reminder that she was no longer in Knotsville's cozy embrace but in the vast countryside of Spain.

"Alright, you woolly wanderers, let's get you back home," she called out, her voice steady but infused with a note of urgency. She started towards the closest alpaca, arms spread in a shepherd's stance. With measured steps, she ushered the animal away from the road, her knitting-honed patience serving her well in this unexpected endeavor.

"Come on now, this isn't the kind of adventure you want," Hazel coaxed, as if reasoning with a wayward skein of yarn that had rolled too far from her knitting basket. Her knack for staying calm under pressure proved useful; one by one, the alpacas seemed to sense her non-threatening presence and began to amble back toward the farm, their curiosity piqued by this friendly human who had taken charge.

"Easy does it," she encouraged, guiding them with gentle claps of her hands. Her effort was like knitting a complex pattern where each stitch mattered—the rhythm of her guidance carefully leading them down the road, past the olive trees that whispered secrets of the land, and through the golden light that draped the hillsides.

The alpacas' soft hums and the sound of their padded feet shuffling against the earth became the soundtrack to Hazel's impromptu roundup. Though her breath grew heavier with the effort, a smile remained perched on her lips, testament to the joy she found in even the most unforeseen circumstances.

"Let's hope this is the hardest part of my visit," she said to herself, chuckling at the thought of explaining this to Eduardo. But for now, she focused on the task at hand, her determination unwavering as she guided the alpacas closer and closer to safety.

Hazel, her eyes fixed on one specific wandering alpaca, that seemed to be straying from the group. She could feel a bead of sweat trickle down her temple. The sun was high in the cerulean sky, casting its relentless gaze upon the rolling Spanish countryside. In the midst of this vast expanse, the stray animal munched contentedly on tufts of vibrant green grass, oblivious to the commotion it had caused.

"Alright, my woolly friends, just stay put," Hazel addressed the cluster of alpacas she'd managed to gather. They hummed softly, a peculiar choir to her earnest plea. "We're almost there; don't you unravel on me now." She chuckled at her own joke, but her heart raced with the weight of responsibility. This was Eduardo's pride and joy, each alpaca more precious than a handspun skein of cashmere.

She approached the loner with the care of threading a needle, conscious that one false move could send it darting into the horizon. Closer and closer she stepped, until finally, she was close enough to notice the intricate pattern of its coat, much like one of her beloved yarns.

"Hey there," Hazel whispered, her voice softer than a snip of yarn. The alpaca paused, its gentle eyes lifting to meet hers with a look of mild astonishment. "You're quite the adventurous one, aren't you?" She held her breath, not daring to spook the creature with any sudden movements.

Instead, she circled around it slowly, her footsteps deliberate and kind. "That's right. Everything's going to be just fine," she continued, her tone laced with reassurance. "I'm here to take you back home."

The alpaca watched her, ears perked with curiosity as Hazel became a shepherdess of sorts, her patience as enduring as the rows of stitches on her knitting needles. And there, amidst the scent of wildflowers and the distant clinking of bells from other farms, Hazel began to feel a kinship with the stray alpaca, both of them far from home, yet surrounded by the tranquility of nature's tapestry.

The alpaca, unfazed by Hazel's attempts at diplomacy, let out a sudden grunt – a sound that to Hazel's untrained ear could mean anything from mild annoyance to impending stampede. She froze, trying to interpret the woolly creature's body language. Was it a sign of trust or a precursor to chaos? Before she could settle on an answer, the alpaca turned tail and bolted, its hooves kicking up tufts of earth as it made a dash for freedom.

"Of course," Hazel muttered under her breath, a wry smile tugging at the corner of her lips despite the burgeoning panic. "Why make it easy?"

She took off after the wayward alpaca, her sneakers pounding the dirt road with less grace than urgency. The animal zigzagged past the already corralled group, sending them into a confused huddle. Hazel couldn't help but think that her knitting group back in Knotsville would have been far easier to wrangle.

"Come on, you fluffy renegade," she called out, hoping to somehow coax it back with her voice alone. But the alpaca was having none of it, charging towards another fence line with the determination of a seasoned escape artist.

It was only when the stray noticed its herd, now huddled together like a tight-knit blanket of comfort, that it slowed down, its curiosity winning over its desire for rebellion. It trotted back to join the fold, leaving Hazel panting and doubled over in the middle of the field, hands on her knees.

"Thanks for nothing," she wheezed out to the animal, which seemed indifferent to her efforts.

Catching her breath, Hazel watched the flock for a moment, ensuring they stayed put this time. She straightened up and clapped her hands, her voice firm but friendly. "Alright, everyone. Time to head back in."

With gentle nudges and soft, encouraging words, she ushered the alpacas towards the pen near the barns. The open gate stood like an invitation to safety, and one by one, the alpacas ambled through. Hazel followed, counting each head as it passed, her attention to detail just as sharp in the Spanish countryside as it was when inspecting stitches on a cashmere scarf.

"Home sweet home," she murmured as the last alpaca entered the pen, a sense of accomplishment warming her like the afternoon sun on her back. She secured the gate behind them, ensuring no more escapades would disrupt the peace of Eduardo's farm – at least not on her watch.

Hazel exhaled a sigh of relief that was as much an expulsion of the morning's chaos as it was a breath of fresh country air. The alpacas, now safely within the confines of their pen, milled about with a collective air of nonchalance. She smiled faintly, her mind already crafting the tale she'd tell Eduardo over a steaming cup of local brew – how she, Hazel Stitchworth, had become an impromptu shepherdess on his Spanish farm.

"One, two, three..." She ticked off each fluffy head, her fingers deftly keeping pace. As she counted, her eyes caught on a cluster of alpacas huddled curiously around something by the fence. Curiosity piqued, Hazel moved closer, her knitter's instinct sensing a pattern amiss.

"Shoo, shoo," she murmured, gently waving her hands to disperse them. The animals parted, revealing not a breach in the wooden barrier but the distressing sight of shoes... and then legs... and finally a torso.

"What the…" Hazel's heart leapt into her throat. There, crumpled and unmoving, lay Eduardo, facedown on the earth, blood pooling around him and through his shirt. A jolt of panic surged through her, igniting her nerves like wool touched by a stray spark.

"Eduardo!" Her voice cracked as she screamed, rushing to his side. The alpacas, startled by the sudden intrusion of alarm into their tranquil world, scattered from the sound, their hooves thudding against the soft ground.

"Help! Help me please!" Hazel cried out, but the vast expanse of open fields swallowed her plea. She stood alone amidst the green and gold tapestry of the countryside, her call for aid echoing unanswered.

Frantic, she dropped to her knees, her hands hovering over Eduardo, afraid to touch, afraid to confirm what her heart dreaded. Her breath came in ragged gasps, the serene rural landscape transformed into an isolating expanse. She needed to act, to do something—anything—but what?

"Think, Hazel, think!" she chastised herself, her brain scrambling to knit together a plan from the fraying edges of her composure. Alone they were, miles from the nearest soul, and it was down to her, Hazel Stitchworth, to unravel this mystery, one thread at a time.

With trembling fingers, Hazel fished her phone from the pocket of her jeans, the screen lighting up to reveal a spiderweb of cracks. She'd dropped it during the frantic chase with the alpacas, but now was not the time to lament over such trivialities. Her mind raced, sifting through the haze of panic to recall the number for emergencies she had memorized before her trip. "One-one-two," she whispered to herself, the digits as foreign as the landscape around her.

"¡Hola! ¿Cuál es su emergencia?" came the brisk voice on the other end of the line, a cascade of Spanish that felt like an insurmountable wall to Hazel's English-only ears.

"Hello—uh—I don't speak Spanish, but please, I have an emergency," Hazel pleaded into the phone, her voice wobbling with fear. She clutched the device so tightly, her knuckles turned white against the sun-kissed backdrop of the Spanish countryside.

A pause on the line, then, "¿Ingles? Okay, how can I help you?"

Her relief at being understood was short-lived as the gravity of the situation bore down on her once more. "I've found someone," she said, her throat tight, each word heavy with dread. The air around her seemed to still, the gentle rustling of the leaves in the olive trees pausing as if to listen.

"Who did you find, ma'am? Are they hurt?" the voice prodded gently.

Hazel's gaze fell upon Eduardo's still body, the man who had shown her the rich tapestry of his homeland, whose laughter had filled the evening air just nights before. Her eyes traced the outline of his form, willing him to stir, to stand, to shake off this horrible stillness.

But he remained motionless, and the truth was a leaden weight on her tongue. "My friend is dead," Hazel managed to say, the words catching like yarn snagged on a splinter. A single tear escaped, trailing down her cheek, leaving a path of sorrow amidst the dust and despair.

"Please stay calm, ma'am. Help is on the way. Can you give me your location?"

Nodding even though the operator couldn't see, Hazel rattled off the directions as best as she could remember, her voice steadier than she felt.

"Okay, ma'am. Stay on the line with me," the operator instructed, a lifeline thrown across the void of fear and uncertainty.

"Thank you," Hazel breathed out, clutching her phone like a talisman against the chaos, her heart knitting together fragments of courage as she waited for help to arrive. “Please, come quickly.”

CHAPTER NINE

Hazel's gaze lingered on the stretcher as it was carefully maneuvered into the back of the ominous black mini van. The dark cover draped over Eduardo's still form denied her a final glimpse of the man who had, until recently, been so full of life and laughter. It seemed impossible that only yesterday they had been discussing the quality of his latest wool batch, jesting about the quirks of alpacas versus sheep. He had been a fixture in her year, the supplier she counted on for the rare fibers that made her boutique, Knitter's Nook, a sanctuary for textile enthusiasts.

She stood there, rooted to the spot on the farm's gravel path, the scent of hay and earth mingling in the air around her. Her fingertips grazed the soft shawl wrapped around her shoulders, one of Eduardo's finest wools, now a small comfort in the wake of his death. Hazel sighed, knitting her brow as she realized she wouldn't be showing off her new finds to eager customers this season.

"Maybe it's better this way," she muttered under her breath, her voice barely carrying over the low murmur of officials at work. Seeing Eduardo's face in such a state might have unraveled her composure, stitch by painful stitch.

The surreal fog of disbelief was pierced as a tap on her shoulder snapped her back to the grim reality of the scene. She turned, finding herself face to face with an unsmiling detective who looked like he could have stepped out of a crime novel she'd read once, complete with the trench coat and world-weary eyes.

"Miss Stitchworth?" he inquired, not unkindly, his voice carrying the weight of duty.

"Yes, I'm Hazel," she replied, her voice steady despite the tremor of shock that threatened to shake her resolve. A knitter by trade, she was used to navigating tangled yarns and complex patterns; this, however, was a knot she hadn't expected to untie.

"Sorry for your loss," he said, though the words felt automatic, like he had pulled them together from a policeman's handbook of condolences. "We'll need to ask you some questions."

"Of course," Hazel responded, her mind already racing ahead, weaving scenarios and possibilities. Who would do this to Eduardo?

And why? She was determined to find out, one clue at a time. After all, she thought with a faint tug of a smile, unraveling mysteries was just another kind of pattern to solve.

"Inspector Martin," the man introduced himself, extending a hand that seemed too clean for the grim work he did. His grip was firm, hands cold. "I'm leading the investigation into Eduardo's death. Can you tell me how you knew Eduardo?"

Hazel took a deep breath, seeking solace in the familiarity of recounting their professional relationship. "He was my supplier," she began, the words feeling oddly hollow as they hung in the country air, mingling with the scent of fresh hay and distant livestock. "We meet annually at the fiber festival to resupply. It's... it was always the highlight of my year."

"And how did you come across his products initially?" The inspector's pen poised above a small notebook, ready to record her every word.

"At the festival," Hazel reminisced, a faint smile touching her lips despite the sadness. "The first year I went, I was like a kid in a candy store. I scouted for the most authentic vendors, and Eduardo—he stood out. His booth was this mix of vibrant colors and exquisite textures. He quickly became my favorite by far. He was one of the first people to welcome me into the community."

"His product is high quality, then?" Inspector Martin prompted, his tone neutral yet somehow expectant.

"Extremely," she confirmed with a firm nod, her pride in Eduardo's craftsmanship undisguised. "In my opinion, it's the best in the business."

"High praise indeed," the inspector noted, the corners of his mouth hinting at a smile that never came to fruition. "So what brought you here today, specifically?"

"Eduardo invited me," Hazel explained, the image of the farm, bathed in morning light as she'd arrived, momentarily eclipsing the darker turn the day had taken. "He suggested we handle our usual exchange here so I could see the farm firsthand and get a tour."

"Is this a deviation from your normal routine?" There was a slight arch in Inspector Martin's brow as he asked the question.

"Actually, yes," Hazel replied, tucking a loose strand of hair behind her ear. "We've always met at the festival hotel in the past. But over the years, we've woven a friendship of sorts. It felt overdue for me to come out and see the place where the magic happens—the place where all the fibers begin their journey. He seemed excited to show me the place and he was going to tell me some news at the end of the week. Something about business plans."

"And what plans did he have?" Inspector Martin asked with a brow raised.

"Well I never found out," she said as she shrugged. "He was supposed to tell me after the week was up. Said he had to wait until after the festival, but that it wouldn't affect our business together."

She wondered what Eduardo was going to tell her. Could it have been about the business going under, or maybe he was going to supply her with something special, some new kind of fiber? Hazel realized that no amount of guessing wasn't going to get her the answers she needed. It was facts she would have to focus on to figure out what happened here.

Hazel watched the inspector's mouth purse ever so slightly before he presented her with a question veiled in congeniality. "Can you tell me about anyone else at this festival who might have known Eduardo?"

She shifted uncomfortably under his gaze, feeling the weight of suspicion that seemed to hang from his smile like an ill-fitting sweater. "Well, there are my friends, Georgia and Leonard," she began, trying to maintain the composed demeanor she held while knitting even the most complicated patterns. "The cashmere supplier Eduardo introduced me to, Paula, I think? And then there's Vivian. A lot of people probably knew him, but those are our only mutuals."

"Vivian?" Inspector Martin prompted, pen poised above his notepad.

"Vivian Kensington," Hazel clarified, her tone frostier than intended as the thought of her rival entangled itself with concern. She let slip, almost begrudgingly, "She mentioned having a fancy new supplier recently, claimed they were the best of the best. She's always doing stuff like that."

"Ah," the inspector said, his eyes widening as if a pattern had suddenly become clear, "so that's why you're here for the tour—to one-up your little rival."

Hazel shook her head, her curls bouncing with the movement, dispelling the notion like lint off a freshly knitted scarf. "What? No, I just wanted to see Eduardo's process and meet all of the lovely animals behind these rare fibers." She gestured vaguely, her hands expressing what words could not—her genuine love for the craft and respect for its origins.

Inspector Martin looked at her, his expression blank as a fresh skein, unspooled by any notion of creativity or passion. It was clear to Hazel that the language of yarn and fiber was foreign to him.

"So he invited you out here to check out the farm just because you're a good customer?"

She could tell that this wasn't going well. And that despite his original indifferent demeanor, this detective was becoming more and more

Hazel's pulse raced, a tumultuous rhythm that seemed to echo the soft shuffle of officers milling about the farm. The air was thick with tension and the faint smell of hay. "Did you notice anything out of the ordinary when you arrived?" Inspector Martin inquired, his pen at the ready.

She shook her head, her curls trembling slightly as she did so. "No, nothing unusual. I didn't see another car for miles. Though, the alpacas were out of the pen when I first arrived. I assume because of the open gate," Hazel admitted, clutching her knitting bag like a lifeline. It felt like admitting to something she didn't even understand. She had told the truth, but part of her wondered if she should've concocted a story. Yet lying seemed wrong, too.

Inspector Martin nodded, jotting down notes in between brisk glances at Hazel, who couldn't help but feel like she was being sized up. "Thanks for the information. Remember, Ms. Stitchworth, stay close by. Don't leave the country until we've sorted everything out. You might not be leaving the country for a while," he instructed, handing her a business card. The card felt cold and impersonal in her warm hands, much like the inspector's gaze.

"Right, of course," Hazel replied, tucking the card into her bag next to a half-finished sweater that now seemed an eternity away from completion. She was already planning on staying for the festival—it wasn't as if she could just pack up her needles and leave a mystery unraveling behind her. But the weight of suspicion from Inspector Martin made her heart sink. He was eyeing her like a hawk.

"Call if you think of anything else," Inspector Martin added before turning on his heel, leaving Hazel with a knot of anxiety forming in her stomach.

"Will do," she responded, though her voice was barely audible over the hum of whispered conversations and the distant bleating of sheep—a reminder of the pastoral peace disrupted by the day's grim events.

Hazel watched as Inspector Martin, with a stoic grace that seemed almost out of place in the rural setting, tucked his hands into his pockets and ambled over to a uniformed officer. They huddled together, their heads bowed in serious conversation. The inspector's coat flapped slightly in the breeze, giving him the air of a disheveled crow against the backdrop of the farm.

Hazel sighed and moved towards her rental car. Her fingers trembled slightly as she scooped up the keys that had been lying next to Eduardo's latest wool samples; they felt oddly mundane in her hand. Each step she took on the gravel path crunched underfoot, a stark reminder of the reality she was walking away from.

"Focus, Hazel," she murmured to herself, sliding behind the wheel of the modest sedan that seemed too normal for such an abnormal day. She turned the key in the ignition, and the engine purred to life. With a glance in the rearview mirror, where the scene of the crime was rapidly shrinking into the distance, she steered onto the road leading back to civilization—or at least, as civilized as it got in the countryside.

As the car hummed along the winding road, Hazel tapped the Bluetooth button and dialed Fiona. The line crackled for a moment before her friend's voice filled the car, bright and unsuspecting.

"Hey, there you are! Was starting to think you'd run off with a sheep farmer," Fiona joked, her voice tinged with mirth. "Having the time of your life without me?"

Hazel's lips twitched into a half-smile, despite the heaviness in her chest. "I was," she admitted, her eyes fixed on the undulating hills ahead, "until I found Eduardo dead at his farm."

The silence on the other end was palpable as Fiona processed the words. Then came the sharp intake of breath. "What happened?"

"That's exactly what I'm going to figure out," Hazel declared with a resolve that surprised even her. The road stretched out before her, a tangle of possibilities and clues waiting to be unraveled. And just like the most intricate of her knitting patterns, she knew she had to start with the first stitch, no matter how daunting it seemed.

CHAPTER TEN

Hazel's feet whispered across the ornate carpet of the hotel lobby, a soft counterpoint to the cacophony of her racing thoughts. She glanced up, and there, like a beacon in a foggy harbor, was Liam, lounging in an overstuffed chair with the casual grace of someone who didn't just stumble upon a crime scene hours before. His presence was a comfort, a reliable stitch in the unraveling edge of her composure.

"Hey, Liam," she said, easing into the chair beside him. It creaked under her weight, a sympathetic groan to the tension that knotted her shoulders.

Liam tucked his phone away and sat up, his eyes lighting up with a mix of concern and warmth that was oddly reassuring. "Hazel," he began, his voice low and steady, "I heard what happened. I'm so sorry. He seemed like a great guy. I was immediately worried about you."

The question tumbled from her lips before she could catch it. "How do you know already?"

"Word travels fast here," Liam explained, his gaze never leaving her face. "The entire festival knows. They've even canceled an event this afternoon because of the incident."

"Oh, right," Hazel murmured, fiddling with a loose thread on her cardigan. The festival—she'd completely forgotten it would persist, indifferent to personal tragedies. "I suppose the show must go on."

Liam leaned forward, his brows knitting together in a look of genuine concern. "Are you okay?"

She managed a shrug, sinking back into the embrace of the chair, and let out a breath she hadn't realized she'd been holding. "No," she admitted quietly, the word barely louder than the soft clinking of china from the nearby coffee station.

In the warm, friendly confines of the hotel lobby, with the muffled sounds of suitcase wheels rolling over the threshold and the distant hum of conversation, Hazel found an anchor in Liam's steady presence. And though her troubles were far from over, she allowed herself a moment of respite, wrapped in the cozy mystery of human kindness.

Hazel traced the grain of the wooden armrest with her finger, the smooth varnish a small comfort in the midst of chaos. She glanced at

Liam, his concerned face urging her to share the morning's harrowing events.

"I went to see Eduardo this morning," she started, her voice threading through the cozy hum of the lobby. "I was supposed to meet all of his animals and get a tour of his farm." Her hands moved to her lap, twisting together as if they were winding unseen yarn. "But when I got there, his alpacas had escaped their pen."

Liam leaned in, his attention fixed on her every word.

"By some stroke of luck—or perhaps it was just my knack for herding wayward things—I managed to corral them back." Hazel allowed herself a half-smile, thinking of the chaotic dance she'd led with the fluffy escapees. "But then... I found him. Eduardo. Just lying there, so still, so bloody."

"Oh my gosh," Liam breathed out, his eyes widening with shock. "I didn't realize you were the one who found him. That's got to be terribly traumatic."

Hazel nodded, swallowing hard against the lump in her throat. "It is. But now, I've got an investigator eyeing me like I'm the villain in a poorly-knit plot." She let out a shaky breath, the absurdity not lost on her.

"They seriously think you would do something like this?" Liam said, surprise etched into his furrowed brow. He appraised her briefly, from her disheveled hair to her sensible shoes. Leaning forward, he lowered his voice, "Wait, would you do something like this? I mean, we just met yesterday, but you didn't try to murder me in the garden, so I figure..."

A chuckle escaped her despite the turmoil inside. "I'm not a murderer, Liam. I didn't kill Eduardo. He was my friend." Each word was punctuated by a firm belief in her innocence, even though the pit in her stomach seemed to argue otherwise.

"So you found him," Liam murmured, prompting her to continue, "and then this investigator came, and then what happened?"

"Then?" Hazel sighed, leaning back again. Her gaze drifted to the soft glow of the chandelier above, as if the answer might be written in the delicate swirls of light. "Well, then the whole thing turned upside down, didn't it?"

Hazel exhaled a troubled breath as she collapsed into the chair next to Liam. Her fingers fidgeted with the hem of her cardigan, twisting the soft yarn as if it could somehow weave the frayed edges of the day back together. The hotel lobby buzzed softly around them, a hum of activity that felt worlds away from her own tumultuous reality.

"I just... left," she began, her voice barely above a whisper. "They told me to stay close in case they have more questions." Hazel's hands stilled, and she looked at Liam, finding comfort in the steadiness of his gaze. "Then I called Fiona—she's my rock, really—and now I'm here." A small smile tugged at the corners of her mouth. "With you, the only person in this entire country willing to listen to my ramblings."

Liam shook his head, his eyes reflecting concern rather than judgment. "So what are you going to do? Just wait until you get arrested?" His question hung between them, as serious as it was absurd.

"Of course not," Hazel said with more conviction than she felt, her head shaking in defiance. "I'm going to clear my name." She squared her shoulders, the action stirring a breeze of determination that seemed to ruffle the nearby potted palms. "Knitters know, when things unravel, we don't give up. We pick up the stitches and carry on. I'll fight until the bitter end."

A laugh escaped Liam, lightening the mood for a fleeting moment. "Then I'll fight beside you," he declared, his words painting him as a gallant knight ready to enter the fray.

Hazel's face fell, her eyebrows knitting together in concern. "No, Liam, you shouldn't—" But before she could finish, his smile halted her protest.

"I want to," he insisted, and there was something in the set of his jaw, a determination that mirrored her own, that told her he meant every word.

"Thank you," Hazel murmured, though part of her still hesitated to involve him further. Yet, as their eyes met, a silent understanding passed between them. They were in this together now, threads entwined in a tapestry of mystery and mutual resolve.

Hazel's fingers knotted together, a physical manifestation of the turmoil brewing inside. "Liam," she began, her voice laced with earnestness, "I seriously can't ask you to help me claim my innocence."

"Who said anything about asking?" Liam retorted gently, leaning forward, his gaze unwavering. "You're not asking. I'm telling you that I'm going to help you." His tone held a note of finality, like a gentle stitch binding off a row.

She sighed, feeling the weight of her predicament pressing down on her. "You don't have to get involved. You should be enjoying the festival, having fun. Don't worry about me," Hazel insisted, her hands gesturing as if she could physically push his offer away. "I can figure this out myself."

"Can you speak Spanish?" Liam interjected, an eyebrow arching inquisitively.

"What?" Hazel blinked, taken aback by the sudden shift in topic.

"Spanish," Liam repeated, slower this time, as if he was addressing an audience at one of his textile lectures. "In case you run into anyone who only speaks Spanish? It's quite common around here."

She bit her bottom lip, a habit when faced with a snag in her plans. There was no denying the language barrier could be as tricky as untangling a hank of mohair yarn without a swift. "No, I don't," she admitted, the realization settling over her like a scratchy woolen cloak.

"¿Hablas español?" Hazel asked, her pronunciation rough around the edges but intelligible.

"Si," Liam responded with a grin, and the word flowed from him as smoothly as silk thread through a needle's eye. "Yes, in Spanish."

Hazel exhaled, a soft sigh escaping her lips. The practical part of her mind, the part that organized skeins by color and fiber content, knew she could probably get along without an interpreter. But then there was Liam, offering a lifeline she hadn't even realized she needed.

Liam leaned forward, his hands clasped together as if he were about to unveil a grand surprise. "Besides Spanish," he said, his voice low and conspiratorial, "I'll also throw in my historical knowledge for free."

Hazel paused, her eyes tracing the earnest line of his jaw. It was as if fate had knitted their paths together with a particularly fortuitous stitch. She marveled at how this stranger seemed tailor-made to be her ally in a moment of crisis. Despite her reservations about involving him, she couldn't help but think that Liam could be an invaluable asset.

"Fine," she relented, the word leaving her mouth like a reluctant puff of air from a half-inflated balloon. "You can help. I could use it."

Liam's response was a smile so wide it threatened to outshine the elaborate chandelier overhead. "What a great way to say, 'thank you so much, you're the greatest person ever,'" he teased, the corners of his eyes crinkling with delight.

Hazel smirked in return, but her next words carried the weight of genuine gratitude. "Thank you, Liam. You really don't have to do this, and remember, you can walk away any time."

"I wouldn't dream of it," he replied, his tone now laced with resolve. The playful glint in his eye shifted into something more determined. "Now, where do we start?"

She thought for a moment, her gaze wandering to the intricate patterns etched into the marble floor, seeking inspiration from the interwoven designs. "Well, there were some animal rights protestors here last night," she began, recalling the fervor in their voices. "Maybe we start with the people who made no secret of their disdain for Eduardo."

"Good plan," Liam agreed, standing up from his chair with a swift, fluid motion. "Let's go find them. I bet they're actually still here."

And with that, Hazel found herself following Liam's confident stride, her uncertainty unraveling as they delved deeper into the tangled web of mystery surrounding Eduardo's untimely demise.

CHAPTER ELEVEN

Hazel led Liam to the side entrance of the hotel, the same spot where an impassioned crowd had chanted and waved signs just the night before. Today, however, the atmosphere was decidedly more subdued. The protestors lounged casually, their presence now as innocuous as a flock of pigeons pecking at breadcrumbs. Some were sprawled on the steps, their thumbs flicking across phone screens, while others leaned against the bannister, bathed in the soft glow of the afternoon sun.

"Over there," Hazel said, her keen gaze locking onto one individual. She nudged Liam subtly and nodded towards a woman who looked up from her phone, her back resting against the old oaken door. It was the sign-holder from last night, the very same who had vehemently denounced Eduardo. "We'll start with her."

There were a lot of signs, protesting all sorts of vendors. But only one of them died last night. So Hazel knew that she would have to figure out why they decided to call out Eduardo specifically, and not worry about the others on the protestors' hit list.

They approached the woman, her sign now lying dormant by her side. Hazel cleared her throat, ready to unravel this yarn. "Hello," she began, her voice warm but laced with an unmistakable edge of curiosity. "I remember you from last night, and I'm quite interested in learning more about your group."

The woman stood, brushing off the seat of her jeans, her eyes narrowing slightly as if trying to place Hazel's face among the sea of strangers. "You're not like some undercover reporter or something, are you?" she asked, her tone equal parts suspicion and challenge.

Hazel shook her head, a wry smile tugging at her lips. "Oh, no. Nothing so exciting, I'm afraid. Just curious is all," she assured. Her hands found their way into the pockets of her cardigan, fingers playing with a stray bit of yarn as she continued, "That sign you were holding—it seemed pretty specific."

"Because he sucks," the woman scoffed without missing a beat, her disdain for the man in question hanging heavy between them. "They all suck."

"May I ask why you think that?" Hazel pressed gently, her head tilting inquisitively. She was a master at knitting together facts, and this conversation was just another pattern to follow, another puzzle to piece together.

The exchange was the first stitch in what Hazel hoped would be a revealing tapestry of truths and motives. She glanced at Liam, noting the quiet interest in his eyes as he observed the scene unfolding before them. Together, they'd weave through the intricacies of the situation, pulling at loose threads until the whole picture came into view.

The woman let out a long, weary sigh that seemed to pull the weight of her convictions with it. "He abuses animals for profit," she stated flatly, her gaze fixed on Hazel as if willing her to understand the gravity of their cause. "That's why we're here. This whole fiber festival is just a front for animal abuse."

Hazel's eyebrows furrowed in concern. "Why would you think that?" she asked, her voice steady despite the troubling accusation.

"Because they all do," the protester replied with a wave of her hand, encompassing every vendor and farmer associated with the event. "They cram them into tiny cages, barely feed them, then take everything—their wool, their dignity. They're left naked, exposed." She shivered at her own words, clearly envisioning the plight she described.

A soft breeze carried the distant sound of laughter from the festival, contrasting sharply with the grim scene unfolding by the stairs. Hazel's mind was a whirl of yarns of different colors and textures, trying to knit together the truth. She knew Eduardo, had seen the gentle way he tended to his flock. The group before her must be missing something, blind to the care he lavished upon his animals. Or rather, had lavished, before his untimely demise.

Liam, who had been listening intently, leaned forward slightly. "Do you have anything specific on Eduardo?" His tone was mild, but there was an undercurrent of curiosity that matched Hazel's own.

"Specific?" The woman's lips twisted into a wry smile. "We've been watching him. He's one of the big names, a major supplier. And we know there's something shady going on with his animals. We protested right at his farm."

"But if you went to his farm," Hazel interjected, her voice laced with a hint of disbelief, "didn't you see for yourself that he doesn't mistreat his animals?"

The woman shook her head adamantly, her hair catching the sunlight for a brief moment. "We just know, okay? You're asking the wrong person. You should be talking to Michelle about this."

"Michelle?" Hazel repeated, the name rolling off her tongue like a new stitch pattern she hadn't quite mastered yet.

"Michelle," the woman confirmed. "She's the one you need to talk to if you want the full story. I'm just here to help hold the sign. We all come from all over, but we've known each other a long time. We travel around to protest this exact thing, so we know quite a bit, but Michelle is the one who puts these things together."

"Thank you for your time," Liam said, offering a courteous nod, though his mind was already turning over the new information.

As they stepped away from the protester, the murmur of the crowd resumed its comforting rhythm against the backdrop of the hotel. Hazel glanced at Liam, a silent exchange passing between them, their next step clear: they needed to find Michelle.

Hazel peered at the seated protestors, their placards leaning lazily against the hotel's side wall as they swiped through their phones. The previous night's fervor had simmered down to a murmur of clicks and soft chuckles. "Michelle?" she asked once more, just to be sure.

The woman with the outspoken eyes nodded. "Yeah, she's our organizer. She plans all of this stuff." As if mentioning Michelle had suddenly imbued her with authority, she stood taller. "She would know more."

"Appreciate your help," Liam chimed in, tipping an imaginary hat before guiding Hazel away with a gentle touch on the elbow. They meandered through the scattered crowd, the atmosphere more akin to a casual outdoor gathering than a protest.

"Interesting," Hazel mused, knitting her brows together thoughtfully. "They seem to parrot whatever they're told."

"True," Liam agreed, his voice carrying a hint of amusement. "I'm usually up for a good old-fashioned system shake-up, but they seem to only dance to Michelle's tune. Should we find her?"

"Definitely," Hazel replied, her gaze sweeping over the group. "But let's unravel a bit more from the others first. We might stumble upon some loose ends."

"Thorough. I like it," Liam said with a smirk that suggested he found more than just her investigative methods appealing.

Hazel's attention landed on a man engrossed in his phone, his back hunched like a question mark on the pavement. "Let's start with him," she suggested, striding over with purpose.

"Excuse me," she began, her tone warm yet assertive. "Do you know who Eduardo is?"

The man looked up, his scoff ringing out before he even spoke. "Of course. Eduardo is the worst of the worst. These farmers..." He waved a dismissive hand, his face creasing with disgust. "We're not standing for it."

"Heard that from Michelle, did you?" Hazel prodded gently, her detective instincts tingling beneath her affable demeanor.

He gave a sharp nod, as if confirming a well-rehearsed fact, then returned to his digital world without another word.

Liam and Hazel exchanged a look that carried both skepticism and resolve. With each encounter, the pattern became clearer; it was time to stitch together the missing pieces of this peculiar quilt of people and information.

Liam and Hazel glided through the throng of protestors like needles through a skein, their mission clear. Their shared look was one of quiet triumph; another clue picked up in the pattern of their investigation.

"Excuse me," Liam said, tapping the shoulder of a woman who seemed to be guarding the stairs like a sentinel. She wore a hat knitted with bold, vibrant colors, a testament to passion rather than fashion. "Could you tell me about Eduardo?"

The woman snickered as if the question itself were laced with irony. "That man?" she said, her voice dripping with disdain. "Eduardo's just another unethical farmer padding his pockets with alpaca wool."

"Really? And where'd you learn that?" Liam's tone was casual, but his eyes were sharp, missing nothing.

"Michelle laid it all out for us weeks ago," she answered with the reverence of a disciple quoting scripture. "She knows things, things others don't. You should hear her talk."

"Michelle sounds like quite the informant," Hazel mused aloud, sharing a meaningful glance with Liam. "And where might we find this Michelle?" Liam added smoothly, aware that every second wove into the larger fabric of their case.

"Here, around 4. She's never late," the woman responded, pointing vaguely at a spot near the hotel's entrance.

"Great, thanks for your time." Hazel's gratitude was genuine, but her mind had already knitted past the pleasantries, unraveling the next piece of the mystery.

As they walked away, Liam couldn't help but comment on the flow of information. "So, Michelle really is our next step."

Hazel nodded pensively, her brow creasing slightly. "Yes, and something else they said... It took me off guard."

Liam tilted his head, his curiosity knitting together a frown as they strolled past the potted ferns lining the hotel's entryway. "What was it that caught you off guard?"

"Did you hear the way they spoke?" Hazel murmured, her voice low but edged with a mix of amusement and concern. "They say 'stripping them bare' like they're talking about grand larceny or something far worse. It's an exaggeration, don't you think? The animals are just being sheared."

He gave a small shrug, the gesture loose and easy. "Probably doesn't seem exaggerated to them. You know how passions can run high when animals are involved." He glanced at a passing couple, their laughter echoing in the spacious lobby.

"True," Hazel conceded, her eyes tracking the gold-flecked marble beneath their feet. "But if they're this intense..." She paused, watching a shaft of sunlight dance across the floor. "Do you think they could have gotten so worked up they'd... resort to violence?"

Liam stopped mid-stride, considering her words. "Hadn't thought of that," he admitted, his gaze meeting hers. "But now that you mention it, if they're this fired up just protesting, I can't imagine what kind of scene they might've created at Eduardo's farm."

"Exactly," Hazel said, satisfaction weaving through her tone. She knew Liam was quick on the uptake; it was part of his charm. "You do get it."

"Hey, what can I say?" Liam's smirk was playful, a twinkle in his eye. "I'm just a good partner."

Hazel's smile was genuine as she settled into a plush chair in the corner of the lobby, its fabric a cozy tartan. "Now we wait for Michelle to show up."

Folding his arms, Liam leaned against a tall, leafy plant nearby. "And how will we recognize our elusive organizer?"

"Trust me," Hazel replied, her gaze intent on the revolving door, "they'll stand out. Like a dropped stitch in a sea of purls."

As they watched the ebb and flow of guests, Hazel's knit-picking mind wandered. Would Michelle be the thread to unravel the mystery, or just another tangle in the skein? Time would tell, and Hazel Stitchworth was nothing if not patient.

CHAPTER TWELVE

Hazel Stitchworth pressed her back against the cool, weathered brick of the old building, her heart thrumming with a mixture of excitement and nerves. Liam Blackwell, her unintentional partner in this impromptu investigation—and increasingly intentional partner in other, more romantic matters—stood close enough that she could feel the warmth radiating from his body.

"So, run it by me again, how is this going to work?" Liam asked, his eyes scanning the quiet street that led to their quarry.

"Simple," Hazel replied, her voice a conspiratorial whisper. "We catch Michelle before she merges with that group of protestors. That way, they can't tip her off about us."

Liam furrowed his brow. "And why would it be bad if they warned her?"

"Element of surprise, Liam." Hazel's tone was patient but firm. " Because people are more likely to show their true colors when they don't have time to weave a cover story."

"And besides," she added with a grin, her eyes sparkling with the thrill of the chase, "I saw this in a movie once. I've always wanted to stake someone out like this."

He chuckled, the sound soft but heartfelt. "Well, it's a good thing you spotted her coming from a mile away. Gave us plenty of time to get into position here."

"Hard to miss a car plastered with signs about saving animals and the big white signs in the back seat, kind of a dead giveaway," Hazel remarked, peering around the corner with a practiced eye. Inwardly, she marveled at her own knack for observation. She'd recognized Michelle on sight, despite never having met her. Maybe she was cut out for this sleuthing business after all.

But then, as if pulling on an errant yarn that might unravel her newfound confidence, she reminded herself, *Slow down, Hazel. It's your first day on the job.*

The gentle breeze carried the scent of nearby flowers from the gardens they had visited last night, mingling with the faint aroma of roasting coffee beans from the café across the street. The sun warmed her face as she leaned forward, ready to spring into action at the first sign of Michelle.

"Remember," she murmured to Liam, her gaze fixed on the approaching figure, "act natural. We're just two people interested in her cause."

"Understood." He nodded, his expression serious now. "Let's go knit ourselves a truth blanket."

"Or unravel a lie," Hazel countered, her lips twitching into a smile as she stepped from the shadows, ready to weave the next part of their pattern.

The cadence of approaching footsteps set a rhythm that matched Hazel's quickening pulse. She exchanged a glance with Liam, her eyes alight with the thrill of the chase. "She's coming," she whispered, the words barely a breath on the wind.

As if choreographed, they peeled away from the sun-warmed bricks of the building, stepping into the open. The woman—Michelle—rounded the corner, her arms burdened with a colorful array of protest signs. Her brows knit together in a picture of confusion when she spotted them.

"Michelle?" Hazel ventured, her voice steady despite the flutter in her stomach.

Recognition flickered across Michelle's face as she nodded, her grip on the cardboard causes shifting. "Yes, that's me."

"We'd love to chat for a moment, about the cause," Hazel offered, her tone light, threading the air between them with feigned casual interest.

Michelle's confusion transformed into a bright smile, like sunlight piercing through clouds. With an ease that spoke of many days spent rallying for her beliefs, she lowered the signs to rest against the wall and sauntered over to a bench framed by the tender blooms of the garden.

"Of course," she said, her enthusiasm as infectious as the floral scent that lingered from their nocturnal adventure among the petals. "What would you like to know?"

"Well, to start," Hazel began, tilting her head with practiced curiosity, "what can you tell me about your cause?" She folded her hands in her lap, the picture of an avid listener.

Michelle's passion was palpable, her smile unwavering. "We're fighting against animal cruelty in the fiber business," she stated, the conviction in her voice as strong as the sturdy stems supporting the roses nearby.

Hazel leaned forward, her question carefully spun from genuine concern. "Do you believe there are reputable farmers who don't abuse their animals?"

Michelle's gaze drifted toward the verdant leaves, a thoughtful silence falling over the trio like a soft shawl on cool shoulders.

Michelle's brows knitted together as she pondered Hazel's question, resembling the contemplative furrow one might find mid-row on a complex cable stitch. "Yes," she replied with measured consideration, the cadence of her voice steady like the click of wooden needles in motion. "There are some people who take great care of their animals and can source things ethically." She paused, eyes softening at the edges as if recalling the gentle touch of wool. "But that's not what we're here to talk about. We're speaking out against the systemic issues—those who don't follow such practices."

Hazel's interest piqued, much like when she encountered an unusual yarn blend that begged to be transformed into something tangible. "Do you know someone by the name of Eduardo? An alpaca farmer?" she asked, her voice even, a gentle tug at the end of a row before turning to start anew.

Michelle's head bobbed in acknowledgment, the nod reminiscent of a purl stitch following a knit. "I was warned about him," she admitted, a frown marring her otherwise serene expression. "He's known for using unethical practices with his animals."

Liam, who had been perusing the garden's flora with an appreciative eye, turned back to the conversation with focused intent. "Where did you get that information?" he queried, his tone light but with the undercurrent of a man accustomed to unraveling historical mysteries strand by strand.

"Through my social media campaign," Michelle explained, her hands gesturing vaguely as if scrolling through invisible posts. "Someone messaged me anonymously and told me about Eduardo's terrible farming. They had pictures of the farm that matched parts of his property. It was real proof. Once I saw all of the photos, I couldn't let it go."

Hazel leaned forward, the motion smooth and deliberate, as though she were closing the final inches between herself and the truth. Her gaze locked onto Michelle's with the intensity of a pattern requiring full concentration. "So, you didn't actually see anything yourself or get information from the fiber community?"

Michelle retreated slightly, as if the weight of scrutiny was a bit too heavy, a tension in the yarn causing her to ease up. "No," she said, shaking her head with a sway like a loose thread in the wind. "It was all anonymous. But I'm sure it was real. It looked like the animals were stored in tiny pens, they were the same ones that Eduardo has on his property, they were stuffed in there. He moves them when he knows people are coming, but the pictures don't lie. They have the street signs in the background, too."

The air hung between them, charged with the unspoken threads of doubt and suspicion. Yet Hazel's demeanor remained as calm as a seasoned knitter faced with a dropped stitch—ready to carefully pick it up and weave it back into the fabric of her investigation.

Hazel's fingers, which had been fidgeting with the light scarf around her neck, stilled as a wave of unexpected relief washed over her. It was like finding out that a knot in her favorite yarn wasn't as tight as she'd feared. They hadn't gotten their information from a reputable source—it was all based on the whispers of an anonymous tipster, not someone who truly knew Eduardo, not someone with intimate knowledge like herself.

"Okay, Michelle," Hazel began, her voice steady despite the fluttering in her stomach, "why is Eduardo so important to you?"

Michelle's eyes darted between Hazel and Liam, her brow furrowing in uncertainty. She seemed to size them up, perhaps wondering if they were undercover activists or rival farmers. The scent of freshly tilled earth mingled with the faint perfume of nearby blossoms, wrapping the trio in the garden's natural embrace.

"Look, we're just trying to understand the whole picture here," Liam said, his gaze lingering on Hazel for a moment before he addressed Michelle. "Eduardo was found dead this morning on his farm."

The statement hung in the air like a dropped stitch, waiting for someone to pick it up and set the pattern right again. Hazel watched closely as Michelle's complexion lost its color, turning as pale as the delicate petals of the daisies that lined the garden path. Her surprise seemed genuine, knitting together a new layer of complexity to their investigation.

"Dead?" Michelle echoed, her voice a half-whisper, as if the word itself might shatter into pieces. "I—I had no idea." She wrapped her arms around herself, almost as if she were suddenly cold despite the afternoon sun warming the back of Hazel's own neck. "And here I am talking bad about him all day..."

"Sometimes, things aren't quite what they seem to be," Hazel mused softly, more to herself than to the others. She felt a strange camaraderie with Michelle at that moment, united by their shock. Yet, even as she sympathized with the woman before her, Hazel's mind was already spinning, weaving through possibilities and patterns that might explain what had really happened to Eduardo.

"Where were you last night, if you don't mind me asking?" Hazel's question was gentle, but it unraveled the composure Michelle had knitted back together only moments before.

"Ah, well, I was at a bar downtown," Michelle began, her words tangling like yarn in a hasty frogging. "It was quite packed, and everyone from the protest was there, so... so people would have seen me."

Hazel's gaze didn't waver, though she felt the itch of uncertainty just below the surface. The kind that comes when you're trying to decipher if a pattern is off by a stitch or if you're just tired. "Alright, thank you," she said, the edges of her skepticism softening her voice.

"Any other questions?" Michelle asked, a hopeful lilt in her tone as if wishing to cast off the heavy cloak of inquiry.

"No, that's alright. Thank you for your time," Liam added, his affirmation wrapping the conversation up like the final row of a project.

Michelle nodded, returning to her colorful array of signs strewn on the ground. She gathered them with an efficiency that spoke of practice, then started edging away from the impromptu inquisition. But as she did, Hazel felt a pull, like a snagged thread begging for attention.

"And he was a good farmer, the best," Hazel called out, watching Michelle's retreating figure.

There was a moment, a single drawn breath where time seemed to pause, needles held mid-stitch. Michelle halted, turning slightly, the faintest shadow of acknowledgment crossing her features. Then, without a word, she continued on her path, leaving Hazel and Liam in the wake of her silence.

"Good job," Liam murmured, placing a comforting hand on Hazel's shoulder. His touch was light, yet it anchored her amidst the swirling thoughts. "That must have been hard for you."

Hazel let out a half-laugh, the sound caught somewhere between relief and resignation. "Yeah, but at least we have more information," she replied, her eyes tracking the shifting patterns of light through the leaves above. They painted the scene in dappled shades of truth and doubt, and Hazel realized that this mystery was far more intricate than any cable knit she'd ever attempted. This was becoming very real, very fast.

Hazel wasn't sure if it was the shock wearing off, or if it was the accusations against a man who could no longer defend himself, but she felt herself slipping into the dread of the situation she was in.

Hazel's gaze lingered on the spot where Michelle had disappeared, her mind knitting together the fragments of their conversation. She turned to Liam, the gears in her head spinning like spindles winding yarn. "I really thought the protests were linked to Eduardo's death," she mused, tucking a stray lock of hair behind her ear. "But Michelle's reaction—she looked shocked at the fact that Eduardo is dead."

Liam let out a thoughtful sigh, his eyes scanning the horizon as if hoping it would unravel the mystery before them. "Looks like we might have to cast our net wider," he said, his voice threaded with determination. "Who else could have a bone to pick with Eduardo?"

A memory tugged at Hazel's sleeve, the image of Eduardo and a younger man, faces taut with emotion over dinner, flashing vividly in her mind. "Actually," she began, feeling the weight of the revelation, "he had a row with his son the night he died. They were practically throwing verbal needles at each other. Maybe he knows something."

Liam's eyebrows rose, his interest clearly piqued. "How do we find him, though?" he asked, his gaze now resting on Hazel, seeking the pattern in her thoughts.

With a shrug that spoke volumes of her 'figure-it-out-as-you-go' philosophy, Hazel replied, "In the wake of the death, he's probably at the farm, tending to the animals. Much like how I tend to my shop after a particularly grueling day." Her eyes held a spark of determination, akin to the one she got when tackling an especially challenging knitting pattern.

"Then we better find a way to get back to that farm," Liam concluded, his tone carrying the soft but unmistakable edge of an adventurer ready for the next leg of the journey.

They walked back towards the main street, the rhythm of their steps syncing like perfectly aligned stitches. The air was laced with the scent of freshly turned earth from the garden beds they passed, a reminder of life's persistent cycle—blooming, withering, and rebirthing amidst all manner of chaos. It was, Hazel reflected with a wry smile, not unlike the cycle of solving a good mystery.

CHAPTER THIRTEEN

The mid-day sun dappled the interior of the car with flickers of light as they rolled through the lush countryside. Hazel Stitchworth sat comfortably in the passenger seat, her hands folded neatly on her lap, gaze fixed on the passing scenery that heralded their approach to Eduardo's farm.

"Remind me again what we're going to say?" Liam's voice pulled Hazel back from her silent reverie.

"We'll just stick to the plan," Hazel replied, smoothing a crease from her skirt. "I'm here to pick up my order, that's all. I still need the fiber for my store."

"Right," Liam said, his tone laced with skepticism. "And you think they'll buy that?"

Hazel turned to him with a small, reassuring smile. "It's worth a shot. Besides, it might convince them that I'm only interested in my goods, nothing else."

"But you're not, obviously." Liam shot her a knowing glance.

"Right," Hazel murmured, her mind already knitting together the possibilities of what they might uncover.

As Liam guided the car into the driveway, flanked by rows of ancient oaks, Hazel inhaled deeply, her keen eyes scouting ahead. "Well, we're here," Liam announced, his statement underscored by the crunch of gravel under tires. "Let's hope Carlos has some answers for us."

With each breath, Hazel felt her heart stitch a steady rhythm. But then, as she peered out the window, her pulse skipped—no cars, no signs of life. Not a single vehicle graced the driveway aside from their own. She exhaled slowly, a thread of unease weaving its way through her resolve.

"Looks like we have the place to ourselves," she commented, her voice quieter than she intended.

"Seems so," Liam replied, parking the car. "Not exactly the welcoming committee we hoped for."

Hazel nodded, her fingers tracing the yarn ball keychain dangling from her purse—a small comfort amidst the unknown. With another deep breath, she prepared to unravel the mystery that lay before them, one clue at a time.

Hazel's hand hesitated on the door handle, the silence of the countryside enveloping her like a heavy woolen blanket. With a determined push, she stepped out onto the uneven gravel, the midday sun casting her shadow long and thin across the expanse of Eduardo's farm. "Anyone here?" Her voice carried, hopeful, but only the soft rustle of the alpacas' shuffling feet responded.

"Looks like Carlos didn't stop by," Liam remarked, joining her side with a casual ease that belied the tension in his shoulders. His eyes scanned the horizon as if he might find answers etched against the sky.

Hazel nodded, her gaze drawn to the pen where tragedy had struck earlier. The alpacas seemed unperturbed, their gentle stomping a stark contrast to the chaos she imagined must have ensued here. "They've likely destroyed all evidence before the police even had a chance to see it," she said, pointing to the ground now shuffled dirt without a single identifiable print.

She had a small amount of hope that there would be something in the ground, a shoe print, a trail from where the body laid. Anything to help them narrow down who might have done this.

Liam followed her gaze, his historian's mind no doubt cataloging every detail for future reference. But as Hazel approached the pen, something caught her attention—a tell-tale sign that someone had been there after the morning's grim discovery. The water buckets, which had stood empty just hours ago, now glimmered full under the sun's scrutiny.

"See there?" She pointed, her knitter's fingers adept at spotting the smallest discrepancy. "Those buckets are filled. Someone's been here to tend to these animals since this morning. And I'm quite sure the police don't know their way around a farm well enough to play shepherd."

Liam's nod was slow, contemplative. "You're right," he agreed, the corners of his mouth quirking up as if he appreciated the absurdity of officers doubling as farmhands. "That wouldn't make any sense."

Hazel couldn't help but smile, despite the gravity of their investigation. It was a small victory—confirmation of human presence—but as useful as finding a dropped stitch in a complex cable pattern. Now, they just had to trace it back to its source.

Hazel's keen eyes roamed over the alpaca pen, searching for anything out of place amid the everyday farmyard scene. The clucking hens and soft hum of bees provided a bucolic soundtrack to their investigation. It was then she caught the glimpse of something decidedly unnatural—a wisp of blue fabric caught in the latch of the gate.

"Look here," Hazel said, plucking the scrap from its metal confines with the precision of someone used to handling delicate yarns. She held it up for Liam to see, the color striking against the backdrop of her palm. "Eduardo wasn't wearing blue today."

Liam leaned in, his brows raised in acknowledgment. "Well, it seems obvious that someone else was here." His voice carried the lilt of dry wit, a hint of shared amusement between them.

But Hazel only offered a half-smile, her mind stitching together possibilities as she glanced at the latch. "No, someone could have given him something, poison, or something. This confirms that this is the scene of the crime. Eduardo was killed here."

“Okay, so we have proof of our intuition then,” Liam replied.

“Yes, but this tells us more than there was an extra visitor. Someone knew how this thing worked." She gestured towards the mechanism, intricate and almost rusted shut on one side.

Liam stepped closer, his gaze sharpening as if he were examining an ancient textile rather than a farm gate. "That is one tricky gate," he admitted, squinting at the contraption. "You'd need some familiarity to operate it, I'd wager."

"Especially if you were sneaking up on someone. Which is exactly my point," Hazel affirmed, showing him the peculiar way the latch had to be twisted—almost like a secret handshake. "I wouldn't know how to actually lock it. It must be someone who's been here before, at least seen how to open it."

"Which could be anyone," Liam pointed out, "including people who've visited or taken a tour."

"True," Hazel conceded, a small shrug lifting her shoulders as she tucked a stray lock of hair behind her ear, her motions as fluid as needles in motion. “But it's better than a suspect list of two." She couldn't help but feel a ripple of excitement; the mystery was unraveling like a dropped stitch slowly being worked back into a pattern.

"Fair enough," Liam responded, his head tilting slightly as another thought seemed to knit itself together in his mind. "Speaking of which, where is Carlos?"

The question hung in the air, much like the dust motes that danced in the slanting sunlight filtering through the barn slats. Hazel let out a soft sigh, her gaze scanning the horizon beyond the fence. The absence of answers felt as conspicuous as a missing skein from a carefully curated lot.

"Good question," Hazel murmured, her intuitive senses tingling. Something about the quiet farm stirred thoughts of secrets tucked away in plain sight, just waiting to be unraveled.

"Carlos wouldn't just vanish, especially now," Hazel said, her fingers absently playing with the yarn in her pocket, a habit whenever her mind was tangled in thought. "It's peculiar that he—or anyone connected to Eduardo—hasn't shown up."

"Perhaps the word hasn't spread yet," Liam suggested, his eyes scanning the empty horizon as if expecting the news to arrive on the wind. "The incident hasn't been broadcasted, after all."

"Even so," Hazel countered, her tone knitting together concern and logic, "as Eduardo's son, Carlos should've been informed immediately." She frowned, her intuition sensing a dropped stitch in the fabric of the situation.

Liam nodded, about to speak, when the percussive slam of a car door sliced through the quietude of the farm.

They exchanged a quick glance, one that communicated volumes in the silence, before both turned their attention to the driveway. There, parked clumsily behind their rental, was a vehicle they hadn't heard arrive, its presence as out of place as a woolen scarf on a summer's day.

Hazel held her breath, hoping against hope it wasn't Inspector Martin come to complicate matters further. The moments stretched, taut as the final rows of a suspenseful pattern, until finally, a figure emerged from behind the car.

"Talk about precise timing," Hazel whispered, almost to herself, as she observed Carlos stride towards them, the plastic bag swinging casually from his forearm.

"Hey! What are you doing here?" Carlos's voice carried across the open space, tinged with surprise and a hint of suspicion.

Carlos halted a few paces away, his expression unreadable as he sized them up, much like a knitter assessing the gauge of a yarn before committing to the first stitch. Hazel met his gaze steadily, ready to unravel whatever story he'd weave.

CHAPTER FOURTEEN

Hazel lifted her hand in a gentle wave, the late afternoon sun casting long shadows across the alpaca pen. She watched Carlos's tall figure approach, his gait easy but purposeful amidst the bleating chorus of the fluffy creatures.

"Hey there, Carlos," she greeted with a friendly smile, her voice carrying over the distance. "Do you remember me from the festivals? I've crossed paths with your dad quite a few times."

Carlos paused, his face unreadable for a moment as he tucked a stray lock of hair behind his ear. "If you're talking about him in past tense..." His words trailed off, and his eyes searched hers. "Then you must know he's gone."

Hazel nodded, her throat tightening at the memory. "Yes, I was actually the one who found him." The words felt heavy, like a damp shawl draped around her shoulders.

His reaction was immediate; his eyes widened, reflecting a mixture of shock and curiosity. "Interesting… What brings you back here?" he asked, clearly taken aback.

Before Hazel could reply, Liam stepped in, his presence grounding like the earth beneath their feet. "She didn't have anything to do with what happened to Eduardo," he said, his tone reassuring. "They were friends. We're just here for a look around the place."

Carlos's posture relaxed ever so slightly, though a guarded veil still lingered in his gaze. He nodded slowly, trying to fit the pieces together in his mind. "Okay, but... why come to me?"

"We have a few questions about your father," Hazel ventured, her voice soft yet insistent, like a knit stitch that refuses to be dropped.

For a moment, it seemed as if Carlos might relent, his lips parting as if to speak further. But then his head shook, a wry smile tugging at the corner of his mouth. "Absolutely not," he said, the finality in his voice leaving no room for negotiation.

The tension hung in the air, as palpable as the scent of hay and earth that surrounded them. Hazel exchanged a glance with Liam, her resolve knitting together with every passing second. They had come too far to take that as an answer now.

Carlos turned on his heel, the plastic bag crinkling in his grip, and made his way back to the quaint farmhouse nestled among the rolling green of the pastures. As he disappeared inside, Hazel exchanged a glance with Liam, her eyebrows knitting together in consternation.

"I don't know, Liam," she murmured, the uncertainty plain in her voice. She felt the weight of the unsolved mystery heavy on her shoulders like an ill-fitting shawl.

Liam gave her an encouraging nod, his eyes steady and sure. "Keep at it, Hazel. It seems you've got a way with figuring these things out."

Drawing strength from his support, Hazel's resolve tightened like a well-cast-on row. Moments later, Carlos reemerged, his expression one of mild surprise as he noted their continued presence.

"Oh, you're still here?" he asked, his tone somewhere between annoyance and disbelief.

Hazel stepped forward, her hands unconsciously smoothing the fabric of her skirt. "We really need to talk to you, Carlos," she said, imbuing her words with all the earnestness she felt.

Carlos's face closed off like a door snapping shut. "Look, I don't really know you folks," he replied, his voice carrying a sharp edge of dismissal. "And I don't have to do anything. Especially not talk about my father who—" His voice faltered for just a fraction of a second. "Who died today."

Hazel could sense the grief that Carlos was trying so hard to mask, the same way she'd spot a dropped stitch in a complex cable pattern. She knew pushing him might cause the delicate weave of trust to unravel completely, yet the need to solve the tangle of Eduardo's death compelled her.

"Carlos, I know this is hard. I just want to help," Hazel said softly, her words gentle as a feather's touch. There was no accusation in her tone, only the simple offer of assistance, as one might offer a spare skein of yarn to a fellow knitter in need.

The silence stretched between them, filled with the distant hum of bees and the soft rustle of leaves in the breeze. For a moment, Hazel thought she might have reached him, but then, like a stubborn knot refusing to yield, Carlos remained unmoved.

Carlos's laugh was short, a brittle sound that seemed to fracture the air between them. "You want to help? You can help by getting off the property and not coming back," he said, his tone dismissive, as if shooing away an unwanted stray. The harshness in his voice stung

Hazel, but she stood her ground like a sturdy spool of wool refusing to unravel.

"Carlos, I understand you're going through a lot," Hazel began, her voice steady despite the tremor of emotion within her. "If you change your mind, I'm staying at the hotel. I knew your father, and I just want to make things right."

He didn't say anything, just nodded without looking at her or Liam, his fingers idly spinning his keys around with a practiced ease that spoke of countless days working the farm. The keys danced in a loop, catching a glint of sunlight before disappearing into his palm again. Then, with a pivot on his heel, Carlos walked away, his gait betraying nothing of the turmoil that might have been brewing inside him.

Hazel watched him until he reached the alpaca pen, the animals greeting him with soft hums. She let out a breath she hadn't realized she'd been holding and turned to find Liam already holding the car door open for her. They slid into the seats, the fabric warm from the sun's embrace.

Liam paused before starting the engine, his brow furrowed in thought. "What's our next move?" he asked, his gaze searching hers for an answer.

"Do you think it's strange that Carlos didn't look sad at all?" Hazel mused aloud, her mind weaving through the pattern of events much like her needles would through yarn. "Not a single tear, no red eyes… A voice crack here and there, but he's already taking care of the animals and it hasn't even been a full day."

"Maybe he's just annoyed," Liam offered with a half shrug, the motion easy like the flick of a knitting needle. "Seems like he was the one to put the water in the alpaca pen. He probably just went inside for a moment to pick up some things."

"Perhaps," Hazel replied, but there was a snag in her thoughts, a feeling that something wasn't sitting right, like a stitch dropped and left to run. "Or maybe there's more to it."

"Either way," Liam said, starting the car with a gentle purr of the engine, "we shouldn't jump to conclusions."

"Of course not," Hazel agreed, though her knitter's intuition told her there was a pattern here they weren't seeing, hidden beneath the surface of what appeared to be plain stockinette. "But we do need to keep our eyes open. For clues, patterns... anything out of the ordinary."

"Sounds like we're on a stakeout," Liam joked, a smile playing at the corners of his mouth as they pulled away from the farm, the alpacas becoming specks in the rearview mirror.

"I'm extremely patient by nature," Hazel quipped back, settling into her seat. "We'll watch, wait, and see what unfolds."

The car rolled to a gentle stop, its engine quieting to a soft purr as Hazel peered through the windshield at the small turnaround, cloaked in the shadows of many trees. It was only a mile from Eduardo's farm, close enough to keep an eye on the comings and goings but far enough to avoid suspicion.

"What's the plan here, Hazel?" Liam asked, his gaze following her pointing finger.

"Stakeout," she stated matter-of-factly, as if it were the most natural next step, like casting on for a new knitting project. "Carlos might have left in a hurry, but I'd bet my favorite needles he'll head out again."

Liam's eyebrows arched, a smirk forming. "I hope you're right. Otherwise, we might be playing a long game of 'watch the grass grow.'"

"Patience is a virtue, or so they say," Hazel responded with a playful glint in her eye. "Besides, waiting is nothing new to a knitter."

Liam chuckled, stretching his legs before resigning himself to the stakeout. "Well, I can't argue with that logic."

Hazel's attention was fixed on the dusty road leading back to the farm, her senses heightened. She listened to the distant hum of insects, the rustle of leaves in the gentle breeze, all while keeping one eye on the path Carlos would eventually take.

"Right, but about Carlos," she murmured, returning to their earlier conversation. "Yesterday, I saw he was arguing with his father. Today? Not a ripple of emotion. That's not just strange; there has to be something else. He can still love his dad and be hiding something."

"Shock can do funny things." Liam leaned back, trying to find comfort against the seat's firm support. "Maybe grief hasn't hit him yet."

"Could be," Hazel conceded, though her tone suggested she wasn't entirely convinced. "Or maybe he's tangled up in something more sinister. We need to unravel this mystery, find out whether he's a grieving son or... something else."

"Let's hope this hunch of yours is on point," Liam said, his voice carrying a note of admiration. "Otherwise, we're just two people parked on the side of the road, hoping for a clue."

"Trust me, clues are like purls in a sea of knit stitches," Hazel said confidently. "They stand out to those who know how to look for them."

As the afternoon sun began to dip lower, casting long shadows across the road, they settled in for the wait, companions in silence and anticipation. The cozy mystery of Eduardo's death was slowly unravelling, and Hazel was determined to knit together the truth, no matter how many hours they had to spend watching the world from their makeshift lookout.

Hazel leaned against the side of the car, her arms crossed as she peered down the dusty road. A faint breeze teased a few strands of her hair free from her ponytail, but she paid it no mind, her gaze laser-focused.

"See that?" Hazel pointed without looking at Liam. "He had his keys in his hand."

Liam, who was scrolling through notes on his phone, looked up, puzzled. "Huh?"

"Carlos," she explained, as if recounting a missed stitch in a complex knitting pattern. "He went into the house to drop off those bags he brought home, but then he came out with the same set of keys to check on the alpacas."

"Whoa." Liam blinked, his features etched with surprise. "I didn't even notice that."

Hazel nodded, a small smile tugging at the corners of her mouth. "Well, I sometimes pay a little too close of attention."

Liam chuckled, the sound rich and warm in the quiet of the encroaching evening. "I think I like that about you."

Color rose to Hazel's cheeks, a soft blush that she quickly tried to brush away with a mental shake. There were bigger yarn balls to unwind here than the flutter in her chest. "A life in prison is at stake. We have to stay sharp."

Her eyes never left the road, watching for the telltale dust cloud that would signal an approaching vehicle. The minutes stretched out, filled only by the rustling leaves and their synchronized breathing.

"Wait," Liam broke the silence. "If there's no one around for miles, how are we going to follow him without being spotted?"

"There are people around," Hazel said, her voice steady as she shifted her weight, ready to move at a moment's notice. "We'll keep our distance, maybe take a few extra turns to throw him off. Carlos has enough on his mind; he won't suspect a thing."

"Hopefully," Liam murmured, scanning the horizon with a skeptical squint. "Otherwise, he's definitely not going to open up to us."

Just then, the faint crunch of gravel reached their ears, growing louder until it became unmistakable—the sound of a car approaching. Hazel's heart skipped a beat, not from the thrill of proximity to Liam, but from the anticipation of the chase.

And there it was—Carlos's car driving by, dust billowing behind it like a cloak of mystery waiting to be unraveled. Hazel's intuition had been right.

"Ha," Liam said, a grin spreading across his face as he turned the key in the ignition. "You're a wonder, Hazel Stitchworth."

"Let's go find out what he's up to," Hazel replied with a smirk, her earlier flush forgotten. She settled into her seat, the detective fibers of her being knitting together with excitement and determination. The game was afoot, and she was ready to follow the thread wherever it led.

CHAPTER FIFTEEN

The sun had dipped below the horizon, casting elongated shadows across the cityscape as Hazel and Liam's car trailed discreetly behind Carlos's vehicle. The soft glow of twilight bathed the street in an ethereal light, a stark contrast to the loud thumping of Hazel's heart, which seemed to echo in the quiet of the car. She could feel the rush of adrenaline coursing through her veins, a mix of apprehension, and excitement tingling her fingertips.

"Any clue about this part of town?" she asked, glancing over at Liam, whose eyes remained fixed on the road ahead.

Liam gave a casual shrug, his focus unwavering. "A lot of these buildings downtown have history," he replied, the corners of his mouth lifting ever so slightly. "But nothing too significant. We'll know more once he makes a move."

As if on cue, Carlos's car veered left, signaling before turning into a side street. "There," Hazel pointed, her voice laced with urgency.

"Got it," Liam said, following suit moments later. The turn brought them onto a bustling street lined with historical facades that whispered tales of the past to any who would listen.

"I just hope he doesn't take us down some dark alley where we can't see what he's up to," Hazel muttered, half to herself, her eyes scanning the surroundings.

Instead of alleys, they were surrounded by the vibrant life of the downtown area. It was different here—less imposing than the massive concrete jungles back home, yet the energy was familiar. People strolled along the sidewalks, laughter and conversation intertwining with the distant hum of city life.

Hazel couldn't help but admire the quaint beauty of the place. There was something charming about the old-world architecture, how each building seemed to hold a story within its weathered walls. Street vendors hawked their wares with boisterous cheer while couples walked hand-in-hand, lost in their own little worlds.

"Nothing like the big cities in the U.S.," Hazel mused aloud, her gaze lingering on a group of friends sharing a joke. "But there's a similar buzz, you know? The history... and the people... It's all so beautiful."

"Every city has its own rhythm," Liam replied with a knowing smile. "You just have to listen."

And listen she did, taking in the symphony of sights and sounds around her, even as they continued their stealthy pursuit through the heartbeat of the foreign city.

Hazel's fingers drummed on her knee, a nervous staccato that matched the thrum of the city's pulse outside the car window. She parted her lips to voice another question, but Liam cut in with a quick observation. "Well, it's not an alley, but it's kind of close."

Following his gaze, Hazel spotted Carlos's vehicle slipping into a narrow parking lot flanked by a bar that had seen better days. The neon sign flickered like a reluctant flame against the encroaching darkness. "Well, it's better than nothing," she reasoned aloud, trying to will away the tightness coiling in her chest.

"We can park on the street, blend in with the crowd. Maybe they won't peg us as bar-hoppers." The corner of her mouth twitched upward, a half-smile born of nerves rather than amusement.

"Sure," Liam chuckled, glancing at her assortment of knitting needles that peeked from her bag. "The knitter and the nerd, we'll fit right in."

Hazel rewarded his attempt at levity with a hearty laugh, the sound more confident than she felt.

Minutes ticked by as they remained cocooned within the car, watching shadows dance across the bar's dingy windows. Finally, with the sky painted in shades of twilight, they ventured out into the brisk air. They slipped through the bar's door, and Hazel was immediately swathed in the cacophony of raucous laughter, clinking glasses, and the earthy scent of spilled beer.

"Thank heavens for crowds," she murmured, relieved yet daunted by the sea of patrons. "But that means finding Carlos is going to be like searching for a dropped stitch in a cable pattern."

"Then we should split up," Hazel proposed, her eyes scanning the faces that blurred into one continuous stream of revelry. "We can text each other if we spot him."

"Good plan," Liam agreed, nodding. His hand moved to his pocket, then halted. "Except I don't have your number."

"Right." A flush of heat tinged Hazel's cheeks—how had she overlooked such a simple detail? She took his phone, her fingers dancing over the screen with the same precision she applied to her knitting. The digits fell into place, one by one.

"There. Now you do," Hazel said, handing back the phone with a smile that belied the worry nipping at her thoughts.

They exchanged a brief look, a silent agreement passing between them, and then delved into the crowd, each threading their way through the tapestry of people, hoping to unravel the mystery of Carlos's nocturnal dealings.

Hazel felt a smirk tug at the corner of her mouth as she leaned in, a flicker of mischief lighting her eyes. "Was that a pickup line?" she teased, the words dancing between them like a rogue yarn slipping from a needle.

Liam's brow knitted together in confusion, his face mirroring the perplexity of a man who'd just dropped a stitch mid-pattern. "What?" he asked, genuinely flummoxed.

"Never mind," Hazel chuckled, shaking her head as she turned away. The joke hadn't hit, and she made a note of it in her mind. She wove through the crowd, brushing past elbows and beer-soaked tables.

The bar was a mosaic of people: a group of young men, their laughter booming like thunder, clinked glasses in a toast; a couple nestled into a dim corner, sharing whispers over a shared pint; a solitary figure at the bar, cradling a tumbler of something amber and strong, lost in thoughts or perhaps just savoring the burn.

Hazel's determination ebbed with each step, the overwhelming din and blur of faces making her feel like she was purling with fog instead of yarn. Just as she contemplated retreating to the relative tranquility of the hotel, her phone buzzed with a lifeline from Liam: *Back door beside the bathrooms.*

Navigating towards the rustic sign that marked the restrooms, Hazel found Liam stationed beside an ajar door, his posture rigid with alertness. Through the sliver of space, Carlos's profile was barely visible, a shadow puppet in a murky play.

Liam's finger rose to his lips, a silent command for silence as sacred as the hush of a library. Hazel edged closer, straining to decipher the muffled voices on the other side. She was met with the swift current of Spanish, her understanding as fleeting as catching water in her hands. Where her knowledge of the language could navigate a menu or request aid, it fell short in the rapid-fire exchange of the unseen speakers.

Her heart played a staccato rhythm against her ribs, a tempo urging caution as they stood, listeners to a conversation woven in mystery and urgency.

Liam's smirk was almost lost in the dim light as he turned to Hazel, his voice a thread of sound. "See, I told you you'd need me."

"Shush," Hazel whispered back with an exasperated roll of her eyes, though she couldn't help but appreciate his ear for languages at that moment. She pressed closer to the door, trying to sift through the rapid Spanish for something, anything familiar. But the words spun and twisted like yarn in a cat's paw—ungraspable.

Liam's wide eyes suddenly caught hers, a silent alarm that sent a shiver down her spine. He gestured urgently with a flick of his hand, and they peeled away from the door, retreating into the cacophony of the bar.

They sidestepped a group of raucous patrons, one of whom was attempting to balance a coaster on his nose, while another narrated the spectacle with theatrical enthusiasm. Hazel could feel the pulsating beat of her heart as if it were keeping time with the clinking of glasses and the thump of bass from the speakers overhead.

The air seemed to grow thick with anticipation. Carlos emerged from the shadows, slicing through the crowd with purpose before disappearing beyond the front entrance. His departure left behind a vacuum soon filled by another figure—a man mountain clad in a suit that strained against his broad shoulders, his eyes scanning the room with professional disinterest.

Hazel held her breath, counting the seconds, her knitter's fingers itching for the comforting click of needles. Only when she was certain Carlos had vacated the vicinity did she give Liam a curt nod.

Hazel stepped out into the cool embrace of the evening, the last notes of a rowdy bar song trailing after them. As the door swung shut behind her, she turned to Liam, her eyes alight with an urgency that mirrored the rapid drumming of her heart.

"What were they saying?" she asked without preamble, her gaze locking onto his as if trying to unravel the night's mysteries there and then.

Liam let out a weary sigh, the kind that seemed to carry the weight of what he had overheard. "Well, when I first got there, the man was all but breathing down Carlos's neck, demanding to know where 'it' was," he recounted. "He kept threatening to rough Carlos up for being late."

"And what did Carlos say?" Hazel pressed, concern knitting her brows together.

"Kept promising he'd have whatever it was soon," Liam said, his voice tinged with concern. "It wasn't hard to pick up on the desperation in his voice—like this was familiar territory for him."

The implication hung between them, dark and heavy like the clouds overhead. They moved towards their car, the gravel crunching beneath their feet a stark contrast to the silence that had settled.

"Gambling debt or something else?" Hazel speculated as she slid into the passenger seat, her mind already spinning with possible scenarios.

"Seems like gambling," Liam admitted as he started the engine, the low rumble a comforting sound in the quiet of the night. "They mentioned how Carlos shouldn't have put all his chips down at once, should've spread it out."

"Wow," Hazel exhaled, a mix of disbelief and realization coloring her tone. "That's... well, it's good information to have."

"Actually," Liam hesitated, steering the car away from the curb. His next words came slower, heavier. "There's more. They talked about Eduardo."

"Eduardo?" Hazel echoed, turning to him with wide eyes. "What about him?"

"Carlos has been taking from his father's farm to pay off these debts," Liam revealed, the streetlights casting shadows across his face. "They joked about the farm running dry of money."

Hazel leaned back against the soft leather of the seat, her gaze fixed on the rearview mirror where the city lights dimmed with distance. The hum of the engine offered a low soundtrack to her racing thoughts. "Woah," she finally exhaled, breaking the silence. "Do you think Carlos was skimming money off Eduardo's farm? And now, with Eduardo gone, there's nothing left?"

"Seems likely," Liam replied, his eyes not leaving the road. "But if Carlos needed the money that badly..."

"Then killing his father doesn't make sense," Hazel finished for him, knitting her brows together in confusion. "If he's desperate for cash, Eduardo being alive would be more beneficial."

Liam nodded, the corners of his mouth turning down slightly. "He sounds shady, alright. But maybe the feud with Eduardo wasn't enough to weave a different motive. Maybe we're missing a piece of the pattern here."

Hazel sighed, feeling the weight of unanswered questions pressing on her shoulders. She glanced at Liam, his profile silhouetted by the passing streetlamps. "I'm going to need some time to think this over," she said, a hint of weariness seeping into her voice.

"Let's head back to the hotel," Liam suggested, glancing at her with sympathetic eyes. "Grab some dinner and rest. You can't solve a mystery on an empty stomach."

"Right," Hazel agreed, though her tone betrayed disappointment. She gazed out the window as they drove, watching the night envelop the city. Her mind spun like her yarn when it tangled—a mess of color and confusion.

The investigation was moving slower than Hazel thought it would. She only had so much time in the country before being arrested on the murder charges. It would be soon, too soon for how little information she had.

CHAPTER SIXTEEN

Hazel Stitchworth's eyelids fluttered open, revealing the dimly lit familiarity of her hotel room. For one merciful moment, she clung to the hope that the previous day had been but a tangle in the yarn of her dreams. But as the morning light began to weave its way through the curtains, the harsh truth stitched itself back into her consciousness: her friend was no more.

With a sigh that carried the weight of both grief and resolve, Hazel pushed back the covers and swung her legs over the side of the bed. She moved methodically, dressing in a soft cotton top paired with her favorite jeans—comfort clothes for an uncomfortable reality. The thought of breakfast lured her forward; after all, a clear mind often needed a full belly to think properly, and today, of all days, she needed every ounce of clarity she could muster.

As she slipped on her well-worn cardigan, the one with the intricate cable-knit pattern she'd completed last fall, a knock rapped sharply against the door. "Liam," she murmured to herself, a small smile knitting across her face at the idea of seeing the man who shared her love for artisanal textiles. But when she opened the door, her fleeting grin unraveled into a frown.

"Inspector Martin," she greeted, barely concealing her dismay. The sight of the inspector's polished shoes and stern demeanor felt like a dropped stitch in the fabric of her morning.

"Good morning, Miss Stitchworth," he replied, tipping his hat ever so slightly. His presence cast a pall over the threshold, suggesting that the day's agenda might include something far graver than scones and jam.

"Morning," Hazel managed, her heart thumping like a drumbeat against her ribcage. Was she about to be cuffed and carted away before she'd even had the chance to sample the hotel's celebrated oatmeal?

"May I come in?" Inspector Martin asked, though his tone suggested it wasn't truly a question.

"Of course," Hazel replied, stepping aside. Her hands were clammy, her mind racing faster than her needles on a deadline. As the inspector entered, she couldn't help but wonder if she'd soon find herself tangled up in a web of suspicion from which there was no escaping.

The sunlight filtered through the sheer curtains, casting a warm glow over the hotel room's floral wallpaper. Inspector Martin stood by the window, his silhouette outlined against the morning light, a stark contrast to the cozy comfort of Hazel's temporary abode.

"Good morning," Inspector Martin said, turning from the view outside with a polite smile that didn't quite reach his eyes.

"Good morning," Hazel echoed, her voice steady despite the fluttering in her chest. "Can I help you, Inspector?"

"Ah, if only it were that simple." The inspector's gaze was appraising as he clasped his hands behind his back. "I'm still piecing together the events of yesterday. I was hoping there might be some other detail you've remembered since we last spoke."

Hazel shook her head, her curls bouncing slightly with the motion. "Nothing beyond what I mentioned before. My memory isn't knotted up; it's just... well, it's been a lot to process."

"Understandable," he acknowledged with a nod. His eyes lingered on her for a moment longer before he continued, "Well then, let's hope the situation doesn't go further if no other suspects come to light. Then it seems like you would be our only suspect."

Her heart seemed to catch on a snag, the words 'no other suspects' echoing ominously in her mind. She felt like she was being sized up for a sweater she had no intention of wearing—especially not one knit with accusations and bars.

"Let's hope," Hazel replied, her smile tight as she tried to maintain her composure. "I suppose we all want the truth to come out in the end."

"Indeed, Miss Stitchworth. Me too," Inspector Martin said, his smile finally warming a fraction as he tipped his hat once more. "Have a good day then, Hazel."

As the door closed behind him, leaving Hazel alone with her thoughts, she let out a sigh. Her appetite for breakfast had diminished, but her hunger for answers had grown. With nimble determination, she knew she'd have to unravel this mystery stitch by stitch herself.

Hazel's hand lingered on the doorknob for a moment longer than necessary, her heart still knitting itself back together after Inspector Martin's departure. She exhaled slowly, the breath unraveling like yarn from a dropped stitch. The hotel room felt smaller than before, the walls closing in with the weight of suspicion.

"Focus, Hazel," she muttered to herself, trying to remember that she was more than just a purveyor of fine yarns; she was also an amateur detective with a sharp eye for detail. Her friend was gone, and the tangled web of motives and opportunities lay before her, a mystery pattern without instructions.

She paced the length of the room, her thoughts weaving through the evidence. The protestors, a tight-knit group with alibis for each other. Carlos and his debts, a loose end that couldn't be ignored. And then there was the entire guest list of the festival—a colorful palette of potential culprits. Somewhere among them was the thread she needed to pull, the clue that would unravel this whole mess.

Another knock at the door snapped Hazel out of her reverie, and she nearly pricked her finger on the sharp edge of anxiety. "Not now, Inspector," she whispered, steeling herself for another round of questions she had no answers to.

But when she opened the door, it wasn't the stern face of Inspector Martin that greeted her; it was Liam, his eyes as wide and open as the first page of a new pattern book. Relief washed over her like the softest merino wool.

"Morning, Hazel," Liam said, a hint of concern knitting his brows together. "I saw our friendly inspector leaving your room. Everything all right?"

"Let's just say he wasn't here to exchange knitting tips," Hazel replied with a wry twist of her lips. "Breakfast might help me straighten out my thoughts—or at least distract me from them."

Liam chuckled, the sound warm and comforting. "I hope today's menu isn't as full of surprises as yesterday's events were."

"Hopefully, the only thing we'll find dead today is my appetite." Hazel's attempt at humor fell flat, even to her own ears, but Liam's presence was a welcome balm.

"Come on," Liam said, his smile a gentle invitation. "Let's go downstairs."

Nodding, Hazel allowed herself a small smile. She grabbed her bag and followed Liam down the corridor, feeling grateful for the company. As they stepped out of the elevator, the soft murmur of the hotel guests' breakfast chatter reached her ears, a reminder that life continued to knit itself forward, one stitch at a time.

Hazel navigated the breakfast buffet with a knitter's precision, selecting a warm croissant and a cup of fruit salad before glancing around the busy hotel dining area. Liam trailed beside her, his plate a minimalist's dream with neatly aligned slices of toast and a solitary poached egg.

"Looks like the early bird gets the... last empty table," Hazel mused as she scanned the room, but then her eyes caught sight of two familiar faces nestled in a corner booth. Like a beacon, Georgia and Leonard's presence promised a safe harbor amidst the sea of strangers.

"Over there," she said, gesturing toward them with a nod. "Let's join Georgia and Leonard."

As they approached, Hazel couldn't help feeling a warmth spread through her chest, a comfort akin to the softest cashmere. She was about to slide into the booth when Leonard and Georgia looked up with expressions that seemed to knit together concern and hesitation.

"Good morning, you two," Hazel greeted, trying to ease the tension with her usual cheeriness. "This is Liam. We met at the festival—"

"Ah, yes, the textile expert," Leonard interjected with a polite smile, offering Liam a handshake.

"Nice to meet you both," Liam said, his easy charm on full display.

Before Hazel could sit down, Georgia's voice, usually smooth as silk, carried an uncharacteristic edge. "Wait, Hazel, there's something we need to tell you."

Hazel stood rooted to the spot, the warmth draining from her face as swiftly as dye from over-bleached yarn. She pivoted slightly, looking for reassurance and found Liam's encouraging smile. Whatever Georgia and Leonard had to say, Hazel knew she wasn't facing it alone.

Leonard's voice was low and somber, cutting through the din of clinking cutlery and murmured conversations like a dropped stitch. "Vivian told everyone that you were with Eduardo when he... passed away."

Hazel's eyebrows knitted together in confusion and distress. "That's not true," she countered firmly, feeling her pulse quicken. "I found him dead, I wasn't there when he was killed." She could feel the weight of each syllable, heavy as a ball of wool after a rainstorm.

Georgia reached out, her hand trembling slightly as if she were handling delicate lace. "We didn't believe it for a second," she assured her, but her eyes darted away. "But, Hazel, rumors are spinning faster than a wheel at a weaving workshop. The people here... they're hesitant to do business with you now. And if they see us together, our own deals could unravel."

The room seemed to close in around Hazel. She looked between her two friends, seeing the truth in their uncomfortable glances. Her heart felt frayed at the edges. With a slight grin, she spoke softly, "Ah, I see. Well then, I'll enjoy my breakfast elsewhere."

Turning on her heel, Hazel felt a single tear betray her composed facade, trailing down her cheek like a runaway yarn end. She navigated between the tables, each step heavier than the last, until she found refuge at a solitary table tucked away from the prying eyes.

No sooner had she sat down than Liam slid into the seat beside her, his presence both unexpected and welcome. "You don't have to say anything," he said gently, his voice a soothing balm. "Just know I'm here. For whatever you need."

Hazel opened her mouth, but no words came out—just a silent thank-you etched in the gratitude of her eyes. She was a tangle of emotions, raw and exposed, yet somehow, Liam's quiet support felt like a lifeline amidst the chaos.

Liam's fork clinked against the porcelain plate as he poked disinterestedly at the pale scrambled eggs. He glanced up at Hazel with a sympathetic quirk of his eyebrows. "You know what," he began, setting the fork down with a finality that matched his tone, "these eggs aren't that good. Want to go to this local cafe I've been meaning to check out?"

Hazel's gaze lifted from her own untouched breakfast—a meal that now seemed as unappetizing as the heavy silence that had settled around them. She studied Liam for a moment, taking in the earnest offer in his eyes. A slight nod was all she could muster, but it was laden with an immense gratitude that filled the space between them.

"Let's do that," Hazel agreed, her voice barely above a whisper. She rose, the sudden movement causing her chair to scrape softly against the tiled floor of the hotel's dining area. The noise felt louder than it was, echoing her internal turmoil.

With a swift motion, she gathered the remnants of her uneaten breakfast on the tray, the colors of the fruit and pastries now dull in the morning light. She dumped the contents with a clatter into the nearby trashcan, the sound jarring in the otherwise hushed room.

Together, they navigated through the maze of tables, each step taking them further away from the whispered judgments and sideways glances. The lobby doors opened with a gentle swish, ushering them out into the fresh air.

The walk to the cafe was silent, but not uncomfortably so. It was a companionable quiet, the kind that spoke of shared understanding and the unspoken promise of support. Hazel felt the tension in her shoulders ease just slightly, knitting together a bit of the strength she needed to face whatever lay ahead.

As they approached the quaint cafe, its windows fogged from the warmth inside, a small smile tugged at the corners of Hazel's lips. The scent of freshly ground coffee beans wafted toward them, and for a fleeting moment, she allowed herself to be wrapped in the simple pleasure of a new day beginning.

"Thanks, Liam," she said, her voice stronger now. "For...well, for being the silver lining today."

"Anytime," he replied with an easy grin. "After all, what are friends—new or old—for if not to lift each other up when the yarn ball of life starts unraveling?"

CHAPTER SEVENTEEN

Hazel's fingertips drummed a nervous staccato on the worn wooden table of the cozy cafe, her thoughts a tangled skein she couldn't quite unravel. She inhaled deeply, once, twice, trying to steady the whirlwind of worry that had become her constant companion. The bell above the door jingled and Liam slid into the booth opposite her, balancing two plates heaped with golden-brown croquetas and a pair of steaming mugs that exuded the rich aroma of freshly brewed coffee.

"Thank you," Hazel said with genuine appreciation, the comfort of the food momentarily knitting together the frayed edges of her anxiety. "This is a nice change from the hotel's offerings."

Liam grinned, a sparkle of mischief lighting his eyes. "The hotel's breakfast wasn't up to par," he agreed, setting down the plates with care. "Thought we could use something more... local."

Hazel shrugged nonchalantly, but the corners of her lips tugged upward. "I don't know, I kind of have a soft spot for those powdered sugar donuts they occasionally serve."

"Ah, but remember, we're supposed to be hating it there," Liam teased, winking at her as he unfolded his napkin with a flourish.

Their laughter mingled, a brief respite from the gravity of Hazel's situation. But as the chuckles faded, Liam's expression softened into concern. He leaned in slightly, his voice carrying a note of sincerity. "Are you seriously doing okay? That must have been tough to hear back at the hotel."

Hazel sighed, the weight of the inspector's piercing gaze still lingering like a dropped stitch in her mind. "It sucks, frankly," she admitted, poking at a croqueta with her fork. "My reputation is taking a hit. And the worst part?" She met Liam's earnest gaze. "The inspector really thinks I'm a killer. It's like my entire life's work doesn't matter anymore... Not when he seems so convinced I'll end up behind bars."

Liam reached across the table, his hand hovering over hers in a gesture of solidarity. "You're not going to prison, Hazel," he said with conviction that was almost palpable. "We're going to find out who did this. We have to."

Hazel looked into his eyes and found a determination that mirrored her own. His unwavering belief in her innocence was the lifeline she clung to amidst the sea of accusations. For a moment, within the quaint cafe walls, the outside world – with all its suspicions and secrets – seemed to fade, leaving just the two of them, united in purpose and warmed by the promise of fresh coffee and unexplored leads.

Hazel's fingers traced the rim of her coffee cup, her gaze lost in the swirls of steam rising like wraiths from the dark liquid. The clatter of dishes and the low hum of conversation provided a comforting backdrop to the turmoil churning within her.

"I'm at a dead end," Hazel confessed, her voice barely carrying over the café's din. "No leads, no suspects... it's like knitting with broken needles." She glanced up at Liam with a rueful smile. "Inspector Martin might as well fit me for handcuffs now."

Liam's brow furrowed, his usual lighthearted demeanor replaced by an intensity that made Hazel's pulse quicken. "It's been a tough day and a half," he acknowledged, taking a sip of his coffee before setting the cup down with deliberate care. "But there's always a way out. There has to be."

Hazel let out a breath she hadn't realized she'd been holding, her shoulders slumping in defeat. "I don't know, Liam. It feels like I've pulled at every loose thread, unraveled every possible skein of evidence. I just..." She shook her head, feeling the weight of despair. "There's nothing left for me to do."

The corner of Liam's mouth lifted in a half-smile, one that hinted at secrets yet to be revealed. He leaned forward, the earnestness in his eyes pinning her to the spot. "There's always another way, Hazel," he said, his voice dropping to a whisper that seemed meant for her ears alone.

Hazel's heart thudded against her ribcage, the intensity of his gaze weaving a spell of urgency around her. "How?" she asked, her voice wavering. "What haven't I tried? What mysterious path have I overlooked?"

Liam leaned back, giving her space to breathe. His eyes searched hers, as if he were sifting through the strands of her thoughts, looking for the pattern that would lead them to the answer. Hazel took advantage of the pause to take a slow sip of her coffee, her mind racing with possibilities.

"They wouldn't call it a mystery if the answer was right in front of us," Liam mused, his tone thoughtful. "Sometimes you need to step back, see it from a different angle. Maybe we're too close to this and we need to look at it in a new way..."

Hazel savored the warmth spreading from the ceramic mug into her hands, letting his words weave their way through her doubts. In the quiet dance of their silent understanding, she felt the threads of hope begin to reknit themselves into the fabric of her resolve.

Liam forked a croqueta, the edges crisp and golden, before offering it across the table to Hazel. "You seem good at coming up with next steps and looking at the details," he said, a warm smile playing on his lips as the aroma of fried breadcrumbs and ham filled the air between them. "Remember the car key incident at Eduardo's farm?"

Hazel nibbled on the edge of the savory snack, her mind momentarily distracted by the perfect blend of spices. "Mmm, I suppose," she conceded with a small sigh, her voice trailing off. "But all that sleuthing just proved that Carlos had one less reason to kill his dad."

"Right," Liam agreed, picking up his own croqueta with more enthusiasm. "But you led us to that. There has to be another thread we can pull, another pattern that will emerge. You're going to find it. I know it."

She watched him take a hearty bite, his eyes closing briefly in appreciation of the flavors. It was comforting, this normalcy amidst the chaos, but Hazel couldn't shake off the weight of her predicament so easily. She set down her half-eaten croqueta and leaned back against the cushioned booth. The police had their methods—interviews, evidence collection, analysis—and she'd mirrored them in her own amateur investigation. Yet, here she was, no closer to the truth than when she'd started.

"Is there anything else to investigate?" Hazel murmured, more to herself than to Liam. She glanced out the cafe window, where the morning light played tricks on the cobbled street, casting elongated shadows. "I've already retraced the steps of the authorities... What am I missing?"

Liam took a sip of his coffee, eyes fixed on her. "What about the man himself? Eduardo must have left some trails we haven't discovered yet."

Her fingers wrapped around her mug, the warmth seeping into her palms. It was a comforting sensation, not unlike the feeling of her favorite wool running through her fingers as she worked her knitting needles. Hazel's gaze met Liam's, and she found an echo of her determination shining back at her from the depth of his eyes.

"Maybe I need to look beyond what we've done so far," she mused, her brain clicking into gear like the satisfying snap of her knitting case's lock. "Perhaps it's time to unravel the yarn a bit, see if any paths lead somewhere unexpected."

Liam grinned, a dimple flashing on his cheek. "That's the spirit. You're a natural at untangling knots, whether they're in yarn or in mysteries."

Hazel chuckled, a soft sound that hinted at renewed hope. Her investigative instincts were waking up, stitch by stitch. With Liam's support, perhaps she could weave together the disparate threads of information and craft a clearer picture of what truly happened at Eduardo's farm.

Hazel's leg bounced as she waved her hand over the laminate tabletop, her mind weaving through the tangle of facts and rumors about Eduardo. The cafe buzzed around them with the clink of porcelain and the murmur of hushed conversations, a cozy cocoon from the world outside.

"Okay," Hazel said, her voice slicing through her thoughts like sharp scissors through yarn. "What if we dive into the digital world for Eduardo? Or at the very least, try to research on the area and the business. A history report on him and his farm might just turn up something new."

Liam's smile spread slowly, like a sunrise over a tranquil sea. "I knew you'd find another lead to follow." His hand reached out, settling gently on top of hers on the table, palm warm and reassuring.

Hazel felt the texture of his skin, slightly callused from handling ancient textiles but still soft enough to stir something within her. Her pinkie peeked out, a small act of independence amidst their connection.

She looked up, her eyes meeting Liam's. There was an intensity there, a shared understanding that went beyond words. Then, as if startled by their own boldness, Liam withdrew his hand.

Hazel echoed the motion, pulling back her own. She offered a shy smile, one that danced at the corners of her mouth, inviting him to join in the quiet joy of the moment. And he did, with a smile that matched hers, warm and bright.

"Right," she said, the earlier weight of despair lifting like fog in the morning sun.

Hazel stirred her coffee, the clink of the spoon against the ceramic mug a comforting sound amidst the whirlwind of chaos that had become her life. The warmth from the cup seeped into her hands as she gathered the courage to voice her gratitude.

"I honestly don't know what I would have done without you here," Hazel confessed, her gaze meeting Liam's across the small café table. "You've been incredibly helpful—and not just with navigating the Spanish and sifting through historical facts."

Liam's smile was like a beacon in foggy waters, bright and reassuring. "Well, it's been an absolute honor to be by your side through all this," he said, his eyes crinkling at the edges. "You don't deserve to go to prison for a crime you didn't commit. Plus, you're pretty great company."

A sense of safety enveloped Hazel, a comfort she hadn't realized she'd been missing until Liam came along. There was a welcome absence of worry when he was near, a feeling akin to the coziness of a well-loved sweater.

"Should we finish up here and head back?" Hazel asked, nodding toward their half-eaten croquetas. She wanted to maintain their momentum now that they had a fresh lead to follow.

"Absolutely," Liam replied eagerly, glancing down at his plate with mock seriousness. "I'm dying to dig into our research." He took an exaggerated bite, his enthusiasm for the task ahead shining through.

"Of course, the nerd is most excited about the homework part." Hazel chuckled, her affection for Liam's quirks growing with each shared moment.

Proudly, Liam nodded, brushing crumbs from his lips. "Guilty as charged. I am indeed thrilled for the 'homework' section of our little investigation."

Shaking her head, Hazel couldn't help but smile. It struck her how integral Liam had become to not only the case but also to her general sense of well-being. With him, even the tangled skeins of a murder mystery seemed unravelable. She knew that without his insight and steady presence, she wouldn't be nearly as close to tying up the loose ends of this knotty predicament.

CHAPTER EIGHTEEN

The click-clack of laptop keys mingled with the soft rustling of yarn as Hazel Stitchworth lounged on her hotel bed, a fortress of pillows propping her up. Across the room, Liam Blackwell commandeered the rolling office chair, his fingers dancing over the keyboard as if it were a piano. The late afternoon sun filtered through the sheer curtains, casting a golden hue that made the mundane seem magical.

"I can't believe I never did a deep dive into Eduardo's business after the initial check," Hazel mused aloud, her gaze fixed on her laptop screen where Eduardo's smiling profile graced a now bittersweet testimonial page.

"Most people wouldn't," Liam replied without looking up from his own screen. "What do you usually do with your time?"

Hazel let out a sigh that seemed to carry the weight of unspun wool. "I knit. Or I'm hand spinning yarn, planning patterns, or... well, thinking about knitting." She chuckled at the thought, feeling the familiar itch in her fingers for the comforting click of her needles.

"Sounds like a regular day for me too," Liam said with a nonchalant shrug, his eyes still on his task.

She laughed, a rich sound that filled the room with warmth. "We must be super fun at parties."

"Parties?" he echoed, finally glancing up, an eyebrow raised in mock surprise. "I don't do parties."

"Neither do I," Hazel admitted with a playful roll of her eyes. "Sarcasm, Liam. I was being sarcastic."

"Right, right," he said, a smirk playing at the corner of his mouth before he plunged back into his digital search.

Their exchange was light, but beneath it all ran a current of shared understanding—a kinship of solitary souls finding solace in each other's company and in the intricate worlds they wove, be it with words or wool.

Hazel's fingers hesitated over the keyboard, her heart tightening as she scrolled through the vibrant images of Eduardo's farm. The alpacas grazed peacefully in sun-dappled fields, their soft, matte coats a testament to Eduardo's dedication. She could almost smell the fresh hay and earth, hear the gentle hum of the spinning wheel from his workshop. Each click was a step down memory lane, each blog post a reminder of a friend's fervor for his craft. Eduardo's passion had been as palpable as the yarns Hazel spun, and now, it lingered on the screen—a legacy trapped in pixels.

"Where are you looking now?" Hazel's voice broke the silence, her curiosity peeking through the sorrow.

Liam turned slightly in the rolling office chair, running a hand through his hair in mild frustration. "I'm sifting through local newspapers online," he said. "But it's like trying to find a dropped stitch in a cable pattern—only the big names surface, and they haven't got a thread about Eduardo."

Hazel nodded, understanding the challenge all too well. "Then I wonder where else I should be searching."

"Perhaps jotting down your memories might unravel something," Liam suggested, peering at her with eyes that always seemed to hold a spark of adventure.

"Could be a good idea," she agreed, feeling a flicker of hope. Writing things out had always helped her straighten her thoughts, much like untangling a skein of yarn before starting a new project.

They both knew the importance of threading together the past to weave clarity into the present. And as Hazel's mind spun with recollections of the festival, the vendors, and the warmth of Eduardo's greeting, she couldn't shake the feeling that a crucial piece of the pattern was yet to be revealed.

Liam reached across the polished mahogany desk, sliding a cream-colored pad emblazoned with the hotel's elegant logo towards Hazel. She glanced up from her laptop, her thoughts still tangled in the web of Eduardo's online presence, and accepted the pad with a grateful nod. Dipping into her purse, which lay open like a treasure trove of knick-knacks beside her, Hazel retrieved a slim pen, its surface worn from the many patterns it had plotted out in her knitting journal.

With the pen poised above the paper, she drew in a deep breath and let her mind unfurl back to her arrival in Spain. The images cascaded onto the page as she scribbled down her memories—a mosaic of sights, sounds, and textures. The bustling energy of the festival's first day surged through her, the vibrant tapestry of vendors, the intoxicating scent of freshly dyed wools mingling with the murmurs of excited conversation.

"Vivian claimed to have unearthed the best high-end vendor," Hazel muttered under her breath, a wry smile touching her lips at the memory of her rival's boasting. It was just like Vivian to turn everything into a competition, even the quest for quality yarn.

Hazel's handwriting looped and swirled as she recounted attending Eduardo's seminar, his words a soothing melody among the cacophony of commerce. Then, a snippet of their conversation after the seminar pricked at her memory—a comment Eduardo had made that now took on new significance. "He said he had something to tell me, it wouldn't impact the business we had, but he had to wait until the end of the week and he wanted to tell me in person." Her voice trailed off as she stared at the words on the page, willing them to reveal their hidden message.

"There's something we're missing about Eduardo's business," Hazel said, turning to Liam, who was hunched over his laptop like a detective scrutinizing clues. "He was planning something, something new."

Liam looked up, his eyes narrowing in thought. "Did he give you any specific details? Because without them, I'm essentially searching for a needle in a haystack here." His fingers hovered over the keyboard, ready to chase down any lead.

Hazel shook her head, frustration threading through her resolve. "No, nothing concrete. But maybe... maybe there's a particular phrase or term he used that could point us in the right direction?" She tapped the pen against her chin, her gaze drifting to the ceiling as if the answer might be written in the stucco.

"Think, Hazel, think," she whispered to herself, an internal pep talk to stir the strands of memory. Then, as if by magic, a word surfaced from the depths—a phrase Eduardo had been fond of.

Hazel leaned back against the plush hotel pillows, watching Liam's face illuminated by the soft glow of his laptop screen. She bit her lip, a dollop of concern unwinding within her. "Try searching for Eduardo's name, then 'news', and maybe 'farm'," she suggested, eager to pull at the threads of mystery surrounding the entire weekend.

"Alright, let's see," Liam murmured, his fingers moving deftly across the keyboard as he combined the terms. He had tried some of them individually with no luck, but not all together; it was worth a shot. Hazel watched the reflection of the webpage flickering in his focused eyes.

"Ah, here we go," Liam finally exclaimed, a hint of triumph lacing his words. The search results materialized on the screen, a digital tapestry waiting to be deciphered.

Hazel didn't hesitate. She slipped off the bed, the cool floorboards creaking slightly under her weight as she moved closer. Standing just behind Liam, she peered over his shoulder, her breath hitching as the article loaded.

The silence between them stretched as they absorbed the words, their two heads close together like sheep huddling against the chill of an unforeseen storm. There was just a single name, but no information, sitting on the page of a law firm.

Hazel wondered what it could possibly mean. A lawyer could be used for many reasons, but this was just on a list of clients, projects worked on, not specifics.

"Look at this," Hazel's voice was barely above a whisper, disbelief threading through each syllable. "He was working with a lawyer?" The words felt foreign on her tongue, as if she were talking about a stranger rather than her friend.

“Maybe it was just business stuff,” Liam said with a shrug.

Hazel wasn’t so sure. “Look through the website, maybe they have more information.”

As Liam scrolled through, the only thing Hazel learned was that the firm specialized in real estate law. “Why would Eduardo need a real estate lawyer?”

“I don’t know, but maybe we should go ask the guy in charge. It says Travis Lopez of Lopez and Associates. The office is right downtown,” Liam replied.

Hazel knew that they needed to see Travis and ask him about the work he was doing with Eduardo. She tried to think of what it could be, but then realized she didn’t want to speculate too much. It would be better to hear straight from the source. Who hopefully would have information that pertained to the case.

“Alright, let’s go talk to him. We’re running out of time,” she told him, as she began to stand.

Liam put a hand on her arm, forcing her to stop in her tracks. She looked down into his eyes as he said earnestly, “You’re not going to be arrested for this crime.”

“You don’t know that,” Hazel said. “I need to figure this out as soon as possible. Or I could be. And then how would I be able to clear my name?”

“Your many friends who would help you,” he said with a hopeful smile. “It’s going to be okay.”

“I couldn’t ask you to do that. I couldn’t ask anyone to do that for me. This is my mess and I need to get out of it.” She was determined to do this before she was wrongfully arrested for the crime. It couldn't get that far. Hazel wouldn't let it.

Liam shook his head. "Stubborn. But that's alright. Sooner or later, you'll see that everyone needs some help sometimes."

"I know that everyone needs help. I'm thankful for your help. I just mean… I can't get arrested. Because I can figure this out. I just need to figure it out fast."

He nodded in understanding. Hazel smiled, finally feeling like they could do this. "Alright then. Let's go meet Travis."

Together, they closed their laptops with a decisive click, setting aside digital breadcrumbs in favor of a more personal approach. As Hazel slung her purse over her shoulder, the familiar weight of it seemed to ground her, a tangible reminder of the tools at her disposal—be they knitting needles or finely-honed intuition.

The hotel room, with its muted colors and soft lighting, felt like a cocoon they were leaving behind. But just as the caterpillar emerges transformed, Hazel knew that each step took them closer to unraveling the tangled skein of Eduardo's fate. And as they stepped into the corridor, the gentle click of the door closing behind them marked the end of one pattern and the beginning of another.

CHAPTER NINETEEN

Hazel stood with Liam Blackwell outside Lopez and Associates, gazing up at the building's quaint facade. The architecture boasted an old-world charm that seemed to wink at passersby, its ornate stonework softened by the morning sun.

"Think we can sneak in without an appointment?" Hazel asked, her eyes flicking to a group of pigeons strutting along the edge of the roof as if they too were there for a consultation.

Liam shrugged, his gaze following a lone leaf drifting down from an overhanging branch. "Haven't seen anyone else enter, so maybe they're not swamped with clients." His voice carried the soft lilt of hopeful speculation.

"Here's to hoping," Hazel muttered under her breath, a quick prayer to the patron saint of sleuths needing a lucky break.

Together, they pushed through the heavy front doors and stepped into the cool, hushed interior of the law office. The lack of a waiting crowd was indeed a good omen, and Hazel couldn't help but let a small smile play on her lips—perhaps their timing was as perfect as a freshly cast-on stitch.

"Can I help you?" The woman behind the long front desk spoke with a professional smile, her tone inviting despite the practiced neutrality.

Hazel took in the reception area with its polished wood and gleaming brass fixtures—all understated elegance. She could appreciate the attention to detail, much like how she ensured each skein in her shop was displayed just so.

"Is Mister Travis Lopez available?" Liam inquired, leaning on the desk ever so slightly. His casual stance belied the intensity of his gaze, like a hawk eyeing the finest thread count.

"Give me one moment, please." The receptionist reached for the phone with the grace of someone who'd performed this ritual countless times. She punched in a number, and Hazel watched the woman's earlobe, adorned with a tiny gold hoop earring, disappear behind the receiver.

Hazel's fingers drummed a silent rhythm on her thigh as she waited, the suspense knitting knots in her stomach. She'd learned patience from hours of unraveling tangled yarn, but this was different—the stakes were personal.

"May I ask what this is regarding?" The woman's question pulled Hazel back, the phone now cradled against her collarbone.

Hazel exchanged a glance with Liam—this was the moment of truth. They were about to pull at a thread that could unravel the whole mystery or tighten the knot even further.

"Absolutely, we're hoping to discuss Eduardo," Hazel said with an assertive nod that belied her inner turmoil. The receptionist's voice echoed down the line, "Regarding Eduardo," before her attention snapped back to them. She offered a rehearsed smile and directed them with a graceful tilt of her head. "Down the hallway, second door on the left."

Hazel felt a flutter of surprise at the ease of it all. She had braced for more of a tangle, but sometimes life surprised you with a slipped stitch that simply worked itself out. As they walked down the corridor, Hazel couldn't help but feel buoyed by hope. This could be the key to unraveling the snarl around her.

The door in question stood slightly ajar, as if inviting them into its secrets. Liam rapped politely on the wood, his knuckles brushing against the grain like a thoughtful caress. A muffled "Come in" beckoned them forward, and they stepped into an office where tradition met tidiness.

"Ah, you must be the ones here about Eduardo?" The man behind the desk unfurled a welcoming grin, smoothing the way for conversation as easily as Hazel smoothed fiber into yarn. Hazel tried not to laugh as she thought about how there was no one else here, yet he needed to clarify that they were 'the ones' here for Eduardo.

"Exactly," Hazel confirmed with a firm nod, her eyes taking in the room—every book aligned with meticulous care, much like her own rows of stitches. "I didn't know he had a lawyer. You worked with him?"

"Indeed," Travis responded, his head bobbing affirmatively. "For almost a year now. Eduardo was a great man." His voice held the warmth of genuine respect, stitching a bond between them with shared admiration for their mutual acquaintance.

In this space of leather-bound books and the scent of polished mahogany, Hazel sensed the undercurrents of stories waiting to be told. Here, she hoped, lay the pattern that would lead them to the truth.

Liam leaned forward, the lines of concern etched on his face like a pattern on one of Hazel's intricate knits. "Did you hear that Eduardo was killed just yesterday?" he asked, voice hushed but insistent.

Travis's reaction was immediate; his head dipped, the joviality that once brightened his features now dampened by a shadow of grief. "Yes," he murmured, his voice a soft echo in the quiet room, "I did hear about his untimely death. So sad, honestly."

The air seemed to thicken with the weight of the unspoken, and for a moment, Hazel held her breath, watching as Liam pressed on. "Could you tell us what you thought of him? What kind of man was he?"

Travis's gaze lifted, eyes narrowing as they flicked from Liam to Hazel. The question seemed to hang between them, laden with implications. "Are you part of the family, or are you investigators?" he probed.

Hazel felt her heart stutter, caught in the weave of truth and necessity. She couldn't afford to tangle herself in lies, not when so much was at stake. "No, we're not," she admitted, striving to maintain the calm she cultivated when facing the most complex knitting patterns. "We're friends, trying to find out who took his life."

The scrutiny from Travis was palpable as he assessed them, his gaze lingering like a careful stitch being pulled tight. "I can't reveal a ton of information. That's protected by law," he said, his tone apologetic yet firm.

Hazel's spirits plummeted, a dropped stitch in her hope. But then, Travis's demeanor softened, as if he were purling back through a difficult section of yarn. "But... I can share the times he was with me as a friend," he conceded. "After the deal to sell his farm, we spent quite a bit of time together."

“A deal to sell his farm?” Hazel asked, unable to hide the shock in her voice.

Travis looked back and forth between Hazel and Liam. “I’m really not supposed to be talking about this.”

“I think you’re going to want to tell us what you know,” Liam replied, leaning in closer.

Hazel nodded. “You know that we have access to the police and we’re willing to tell them about you and Eduardo spending quite a bit of time together outside of your duties as his lawyer.”

She kept the part about her knowing the police because she was a suspect in the case to herself. That kind of information wasn’t going to help her here.

“I didn’t do anything, so I’m not afraid of the police,” Travis replied as he sat up straighter than before.

She smirked, knowing that she had just the right words on the tip of her tongue. “Just because you didn’t do anything, doesn’t mean they won’t try to pin this on you. You have to admit that a friendship with a client can cause some complications.”

Travis adamantly shook his head. “Not with ours. We were very careful to keep our work and personal relationships separate.”

“But the police don’t know that. No one knows that besides you and a man who can’t explain that to the cops,” Liam said, after he clearly learned what Hazel was trying to do.

Travis rushed out his words nervously. “Okay, listen. All I can say is that Eduardo had a buyer, for a huge majority of the property. He was getting ready for retirement and wanted the money to work less and enjoy the rest of his life. He was downsizing.”

“What about his clients? His business was going so well,” Hazel said, still trying to absorb the shock of the news.

“He was letting them down at the festival. He said he was going to keep some of the big clients, but he was throwing out the accounts of everyone else,” Travis explained.

Hazel wondered if she was considered a large-scale client. She did buy a lot of material from him, but her shop was relatively small compared to some of the other businesses at the festival. But then why would Eduardo invite her to the farm to check things out if he was going to stop supplying to her? No, she had to be in the group that he was going to continue working with.

"Did he ever mention why he decided to sell?" Hazel ventured, her voice steady even as her hands itched to fidget with the yarn she always kept at hand for moments just like this.

"Ah, well, I can't say much." Travis leaned back, his chair creaking softly under the shift of weight. "But Eduardo mentioned he just wanted to downsize. Not just the farm, but his life. He wanted a simpler life. The papers were all ready, the signing was supposed to take place just after the festival."

Hazel nodded understandingly, filing away each snippet of conversation like precious skeins of rare wool, each one potentially the key to unraveling the mystery surrounding Eduardo's death.

“Why didn’t he tell me about this?” Hazel asked. “Or why didn’t he tell anyone?”

“I told him not to say anything until the papers were signed. It’s never a done deal until then. You don’t want clients to get ahead of themselves and start planning things when anything could fall through at any time,” the man on the other side of the desk explained.

"Right," Hazel said, her mind knitting together the pieces of information. "Okay, but did he ever express concern over anyone... perhaps being upset with him?"

Travis shook his head, causing the overhead light to glint off his polished bald spot, an island in a sea of salt-and-pepper hair. "No, Eduardo never mentioned having an enemy. Our chats were always cordial, friendly."

"Okay then," Hazel persisted gently, "was there anything he told you about his business, aside from selling part of the land?"

For a moment, Travis's face became as still as a pond with no breeze to disturb it. Then, with a hand reaching up to stroke his chin thoughtfully, he replied, "Actually, yes. One night at the bar, he confided in me. He was just really nervous about having to turn people away. That they would be angry with him for stopping his supply to them."

"Really?" Hazel's interest was piqued. That many rejections could weave a tapestry of potential grudges.

Liam leaned forward in his chair, the curiosity evident in his eyes. "So how did Eduardo feel about having to turn people away? Did anyone's reaction stand out as, well, over the top?"

Travis paused, tilting his head as if sifting through a mental catalog of conversations. "Eduardo didn't drop any names, but he did share that it weighed on him, having to say no. He cherished his regulars and wanted to maintain those relationships. He yearned for that simpler life again—less business, less hassle, just contentment with what was already in his day-to-day." Travis's voice softened with remembrance. "He mentioned that this upcoming festival would be his curtain call as a vendor. After that, he just wanted to champion the good folks in the industry. He would only work with the people he really cared about."

Hazel nodded, her lips curving in a soft smile at the image of Eduardo, the advocate. "That sounds like him," she said. "Thank you for your time, Mr. Lopez. We won't make any more of a mess of your afternoon."

Travis stood and extended a hand, which Hazel shook warmly. "I'm glad someone's looking into this. Eduardo was a good man—a rare breed. I didn't do it, but I'd like to know who did. Eduardo didn't deserve this."

"Indeed, he was," Hazel agreed, her voice tinged with respect.

They exited Travis's office, their footsteps quiet against the plush carpet. As they passed the front desk, Hazel offered a polite, "Goodbye" to the receptionist, who responded with a practiced smile.

Once outside, Liam's gaze locked onto Hazel's with an unspoken question. "What now?" he asked, the hint of adventure knitting itself between his brows.

Hazel drew in a deep breath, the fresh air filling her lungs as the gears in her mind spun with newfound clarity. "Actually," she began, a spark lighting up her eyes, "I think I caught something during our talk with Travis that might just lead us to something—or someone—important."

Liam's eyebrows arched inquisitively as they stepped from the cool shadow of Lopez and Associates into the golden afternoon light. "What?" he asked, a note of excitement threading his voice.

Hazel pulled her cardigan tighter around her, the autumn chill nipping at her cheeks as she mulled over the puzzle pieces they'd collected. The murmur of the city wrapped around them, but her mind was back in the quiet of Travis's office, sifting through every word, every intonation.

"We need to go back to the hotel," she said with measured certainty, her gaze flicking to Liam's. "I need to double-check something, but if what I'm thinking is true..." She trailed off, the gravity of her realization anchoring her next words. "I'm pretty sure I know who killed Eduardo."

"Seriously?" Liam's voice was a mix of astonishment and admiration. A breeze tousled his hair, adding a disheveled charm to the moment. He looked like one of those rugged explorers from the novels she secretly devoured on quiet nights at Knitter's Nook.

"Like a dropped stitch that unravels an entire scarf, there's just one detail that stands out." Hazel couldn't help but let a small smirk play at the corner of her lips, despite the grim topic. She started walking, her steps brisk and purposeful.

Liam fell into step beside her, his long strides matching hers. "And you're going to leave me on pins and needles like this?"

"Only for a short while, I promise," she replied, the corners of her eyes crinkling with mirth. "But it's best to cross our 't's and knit our 'p's before we make any bold accusations."

"Knit our 'p's?" he echoed, chuckling at her turn of phrase.

"Something like that," she said with a laugh. Her humor was a soft yarn wrapping itself around the sharp edges of their investigation, offering a bit of comfort as they delved deeper into the mystery.

The pair navigated the bustling streets, their shadows stretching long on the sidewalk as the sun began its descent. The familiar sights of the city were a cozy backdrop to their sleuthing, each boutique and café a stitch in the fabric of their current adventure.

"Back to the hotel then," Liam said as they approached the corner where they would hail a cab. "I can't wait to see what you've unraveled."

"Let's hope it's not just a tangle of loose ends," Hazel responded, her eyes gleaming with determination. She was ready to reveal what had happened to Eduardo.

CHAPTER TWENTY

Hazel Stitchworth stood, her hand poised in mid-air just before the door of room 408, gathering the skein of her courage. The mahogany panel loomed before her like a final stitch in a complex pattern that she was about to unravel. With a deep breath that did little to steady her racing heart but much to steel her resolve, she rapped smartly on the wood. The click-clack of her knuckles against the door echoed down the hotel corridor, sounding to her as final as the snip of yarn at the end of a project.

The door swung open, and there stood Vivian Kensington, sleek as ever in a cashmere cardigan that Hazel wouldn't mind having in her own collection—if it hadn't been produced by her rival's less-than-traditional methods.

"What the heck are you doing here?" Vivian's voice was sharp, like the point of a size zero needle.

"Can I come in?" Hazel asked, a smile playing at the corners of her mouth. She hoped it didn't look as forced as it felt.

Vivian scoffed, folding her arms in a way that made her bracelets clink—a chorus of tiny gavels passing judgment. "Not until you tell me what you're here for."

As Vivian scanned the hallway behind Hazel, her gaze was searching, suspicious—probably expecting a flock of police or an ambush of irate knitters. But the corridor remained empty save for the occasional waft of artificially freshened air from a vent.

"I'd like to talk in private," Hazel said, letting her smile widen just a touch more. "And I think you'd probably prefer it that way too."

With a scowl that could sour milk—or at least tangle a perfectly good hank of merino—Vivian stepped aside. Hazel crossed the threshold into the hotel room, each step feeling like a purl in a sea of knits, unfamiliar yet crucial to the pattern.

"Fine," Vivian muttered, closing the door with a decisive click.

Hazel took a moment to appreciate the symmetry between their rooms; the same plush carpet underfoot that threatened to swallow her sensible flats whole, the same artwork on the walls striving for elegance but achieving mere blandness. Yet, even among the similarities, Hazel's detective senses picked up on the differences—the tension in the air, the slight disarray of papers on Vivian's desk, an atmosphere charged with anticipation.

"Make it quick, Hazel." Vivian's tone was all business now, brisk as the snap of a ball winder cutting through tangled yarn. "I have things to do."

Hazel's eyes twinkled with a secret knowledge, and her voice held the soft confidence of someone who had pieced together the puzzle, one stitch at a time. "Oh, I don't think this will take long at all."

Hazel perched on the edge of the hotel bed, its quilted comforter as pristine and untouched as her own. Her fingers brushed against the fabric, smoothing out an imaginary wrinkle as she took in Vivian's poised figure seated across from her on the office chair. The room mirrored her own in almost every way, yet it felt like entering a parallel universe—a place where coziness was replaced with a cold undercurrent.

"Alright, what do you want, Hazel?" Vivian demanded, her voice as sharp as pointed knitting needles. "Why did you barge in here?"

"Ever had any contact with Eduardo?" Hazel asked, her tone casual but her gaze unwavering.

Vivian let out a huff that sounded suspiciously like restrained amusement. "Of course, he’s a popular vendor here. I've spoken to him before."

"Recently?" Hazel pressed, watching as Vivian's shoulders rose in a nonchalant shrug.

"Maybe," Vivian replied, with the air of someone discussing the weather rather than a possible connection to a crime. "But why does it matter?"

"Because he was murdered," Hazel said, the words hanging between them like a dropped stitch waiting to be picked up.

Vivian scoffed, leaning back in her chair as if the gravity of the situation couldn't possibly touch her. "Yeah, probably by you."

"Come on, Vivian. You know that's not true," Hazel countered smoothly, her smile faint but present. "You're not exactly known for keeping quiet. Gossip is more your style, isn't it?"

With that, Hazel's eyes remained fixed on Vivian, looking for the telltale snag that would unravel this tightly wound facade.

Vivian's eyes narrowed into slits, a warning sign that Hazel had seen before when her rival was ready to pounce. "Yeah, but only about you," she retorted, as if gossip were an exclusive luxury item in her collection.

"Is that so?" Hazel replied, her voice light, as if they were discussing an intriguing knitting pattern rather than veiled accusations. "But then again, I heard you boasting about a new, fancy supplier for your wool. Quite the catch, isn't it?"

"Indeed," Vivian nodded curtly, as if confirming the quality of a high-grade cashmere. "The contract is already set up."

"Mind if I take a peek at that contract? Just for...curiosity's sake," Hazel asked, her eyebrows arching with feigned innocence.

Vivian crossed her arms tightly over her chest, as if shielding herself with an invisible shield of fine merino yarn. "I don't have to prove anything to you," she snapped.

Hazel tilted her head slightly, giving her best impression of a concerned confidante. "Well, I'd wager that it has Eduardo's name on it." She watched carefully, waiting for the telltale twitch or shift in Vivian's posture.

"What?" Vivian scooted forward in her chair, dropping her arms to her sides, her demeanor changing from defensive to genuinely flustered. This was the moment Hazel had been stitching together in her mind.

"Your big dealer," Hazel continued, her tone even, "was going to be Eduardo, wasn't that right?"

"No, it wasn't," Vivian denied quickly, too quickly. Her voice held the flatness of a poorly blocked sweater, lacking any real conviction.

"Then show me the contract," Hazel pressed, her request hanging in the air like the delicate pause between knit and purl.

Vivian's face hardened, the way Hazel's own did when she encountered a particularly stubborn knot in her yarn. "How could you come in here and think—how dare you think I had anything to do with this?"

Hazel noted the defensiveness, the crack in Vivian's polished exterior revealing the frayed edges beneath. It was all in the details, after all, and Hazel Stitchworth never missed a stitch.

Hazel leaned in, her eyes unyielding as she locked onto Vivian's uneasy gaze. "I know you did this," she said with a calm certainty that belied the gravity of her accusation. "You wanted Eduardo all to yourself, his exquisite fibers spun exclusively for your so-called artisanal line. He turned you down, and oh, how that must have pricked at your pride. Eduardo wouldn't have worked with you because he was downsizing his business. Which means that you probably were just notified that he wasn't going to work with you anymore, and you were furious."

Vivian's head shook with a vehemence that set her sleek bob swaying, her porcelain features tight with indignation. "No, I wouldn't... I couldn't possibly... You're being utterly ridiculous, Hazel." But the tremor in her voice betrayed her, like a dropped stitch in an otherwise flawless pattern.

"Then the contract," Hazel pressed on, her tone firm but not unkind, like a seasoned knitter instructing a novice. "It's the only thing that could unravel this mess and prove your innocence."

"Absolutely not," Vivian retorted, her refusal echoing through the room, bouncing off the impersonal hotel walls adorned with bland prints of abstract art.

"Fine." Hazel straightened, a wry smile playing at the corners of her lips. "If you won't show me, then they will."

As if cued by the drama of the moment, the door swung open, revealing Inspector Martin, his silhouette framed by the hallway lights. A small entourage of officers clustered behind him, their presence filling the doorway with an air of authority.

"Vivian Kensington," Inspector Martin announced, stepping into the room, his voice gravely official. "You are under arrest."

"Arrest?" Vivian parroted, her composure splintering like cheap acrylic yarn. "You don't have any proof!"

"Actually, we have a warrant," he replied coolly, holding up the document for her to see, "based on evidence presented by Miss Stitchworth here."

Hazel offered the inspector a sheepish grin. "Sorry, Inspector Martin. I knitted together as much of the case as I could, but she's quite the slippery skein."

Inspector Martin barely acknowledged Hazel's attempt at levity. His focus was solely on Vivian now, who stood as rigid as a pair of unused knitting needles. The officers began to filter into the room past the inspector, their movements methodical as they prepared to carry out their duties.

"Let's go, Miss Kensington," one officer said, reaching for Vivian's arm.

"Please, you're making a mistake!" Vivian's voice unraveled into desperation as she was ushered out the door, leaving Hazel alone amidst the unraveling of a meticulously crafted lie.

With an air of disinterest, Inspector Martin turned his back to Hazel as she stood by the bed, her hands clasped together in a blend of anxiety and anticipation. The other officers, meanwhile, were like moths to a flame around Vivian's desk and luggage, their hands shuffling through papers and personal effects with swift professionalism. The hotel room, once a sanctuary of privacy, was now exposed—every drawer and pocket a subject of scrutiny.

"Here," one officer announced, his voice slicing through the tense atmosphere. He held up a document triumphantly, much like Hazel would hold a finished knitting project after countless hours of work. Hazel leaned forward, her eyes catching sight of the contract—a tangible piece of evidence that could stitch together the final loose ends of the case. It was between Eduardo and Vivian, its lines and clauses printed neatly, yet starkly missing Eduardo's confirming signature.

"Wait, I'm innocent!" Vivian protested, her sleek exterior fraying at the edges as Inspector Martin's firm grasp held her arm. "This wasn't what it looks like."

But her plea hung limp in the air, like yarn without tension, as Inspector Martin steered her toward the door. The policemen formed a somber procession behind them, leaving Hazel alone amidst the tangles of the investigation's aftermath.

She exhaled slowly, feeling the weight of her suspicions and discoveries lift slightly with each breath. But before the door could click shut on the chapter of turmoil, a foot wedged itself against it, halting its closure.

"Excellent work, Hazel." Liam stepped into the room, a smile on his face that seemed to knit warmth back into the space. His eyes reflected genuine admiration, the kind that added a cozy texture to the ambiance.

"Thank you," Hazel replied, a small laugh escaping her lips as she smoothed down her shirt—a nervous habit after moments of tension. "I'm just relieved it's over, and that we figured it out."

Liam's gaze lingered on her as he crossed the room to stand closer. "And how did you manage to unravel this mystery?" His voice held a hint of playful curiosity, the kind that had first drawn Hazel to him amidst the vibrant skeins of fibers and textiles at the festivals they both frequented.

Hazel shrugged modestly, her hand brushing a stray lock of hair behind her ear. "Just following the pattern until all the pieces fell into place."

Hazel perched on the edge of a plush armchair, its fabric a soft whisper against her jeans as she watched Liam lean against the mahogany desk, his casual stance at odds with the gravity of the situation they had just weathered. The room was steeped in the aftermath of discovery; the lingering scent of urgency still clung to the air like static.

"Everything fell into place when the attorney mentioned Eduardo's rejections," Hazel began, tracing a pattern on the chair's armrest with her finger. "I knew that Vivian was bragging about her new deal with a big name, and if he were to turn her down or tell her that he wasn't able to provide for her anymore, she'd be furious."

Liam's eyes brightened, appreciative of her metaphor. "That's quick thinking," he praised. "So now that we've figured this out and it's over, what's next for you?"

Hazel glanced around the disheveled room, the strewn papers a testament to the chaos of the day. With a nonchalant shrug, she said, "I suppose I'll try to enjoy my last day here tomorrow. Maybe visit the local market, see if there are any unique fibers to be found."

"Speaking of unique finds," Liam said with a slight tilt of his head, a playful glimmer dancing in his eyes, "even though my services as a translator won't be needed, would you mind if I tagged along? I promise not to get lost in translation."

A genuine smile tugged at the corners of Hazel's lips, and she nodded, her heart knitting a few hopeful stitches at his invitation. "Absolutely, Liam. I'd like that."

CHAPTER TWENTY ONE

Hazel zipped the final compartment of her suitcase with a satisfying swish, stepping back to survey the room that had been her temporary knitting sanctuary. The space was devoid of the usual yarn chaos, her needles and skeins neatly tucked away, ready for their next adventure. Just as she gave the room one last nostalgic glance, a soft rap echoed against the door.

"Come in," she called, adjusting her cardigan.

Liam's head popped around the door, his usual scholarly look softened by a hint of reluctance. "Ready for breakfast?" he asked, his eyes briefly scanning the barren room.

"Ah, but I remember you're not the biggest fan of the hotel buffet," Hazel teased, the corner of her mouth curling up. "Think you can manage one last time?"

Liam considered this, running a hand through his hair before offering a nod. "For you? I suppose I can endure. Especially since you requested it so diplomatically."

"Charm always wins, doesn't it?" Hazel chuckled, and together they made their way down the corridor.

The elevator hummed gently as it descended, and when the doors slid open, they were greeted by the mingled aromas of coffee and sizzling bacon wafting from the breakfast area. They stepped out into the busy lobby, but before they could take more than a few paces toward the buffet, a voice pierced the morning hubbub.

"Hazel!"

She turned to find Leonard and Georgia approaching, their expressions a blend of relief and awkwardness. Georgia's smile was tentative as she spoke. "We've been hoping to bump into you. We...owe you an apology about the other day."

"Still convinced I have a secret life as a criminal mastermind?" Hazel cocked an eyebrow, unable to resist a playful jab.

Leonard shook his head vigorously, his round cheeks reddening. "Of course not! It's just, you understand—we were concerned about our shops. But we should've known better. Should've supported you."

“You really thought I was a murderer,” Hazel reminded them, sternly. “I know I like to make fun, but that really hurt my feelings.

And you left me out to dry. Imagine I did go to jail or end up needing you to help me. You wouldn't have been there. I thought we were better friends than that."

"Absolutely," Georgia agreed, mustering a hopeful smile. "And we truly are sorry. Nothing we can say will make up for it, but we hope it's the start of something."

"You're right," Leonard affirmed, his voice steady but not without empathy. "Friends don't turn on each other over a rumor and a little business scare."

"We've learned our lesson, that's for sure," Georgia added, her gaze lingering on Hazel as if seeking an invisible thread of forgiveness.

"I'll consider your apologies," Hazel replied with a noncommittal nod, watching the pair shuffle away, heads bowed in a silent plea for absolution. They were her good friends, but they turned on her. It hurt more that it was someone who was close to her, rather than a stranger, like Vivian. That's when she felt the most alone.

Liam waited until they were out of earshot. "You okay? That was pretty intense."

"Intensity is warranted," Hazel said, her eyes following the retreating figures. "They were quick to judge, and slower to make amends. That stings."

"Are you going to forgive them?" Liam asked, his tone gentle, as they queued up for breakfast. The smell of roasted coffee beans mingled with the warm scent of fresh pastries, creating an inviting atmosphere that belied the complexity of their conversation.

"Eventually," she mused, her gaze softening. "Their hearts seem to be in the right place, even if their actions strayed." Hazel picked up a plate, her motions automatic as the puzzle pieces of the past days' events continued to knit together in her mind.

"Speaking of misplaced actions," she began, turning to Liam with furrowed brows. "If Vivian knew Eduardo wasn't signing with her, why would she eliminate him? What purpose would it serve?"

Liam reached for a buttery croissant, pausing mid-reach. "Perhaps it's the old yarn—'if I can't have him, no one can'?"

"Too simple," Hazel countered, shaking her head. "Vivian's ambition is cut from a different cloth. She wouldn't unravel her own plans over something so... petty."

"True," Liam conceded, placing the croissant on his plate and giving her a thoughtful look. "There's likely more to this tangle than we've unwound."

"Exactly." Hazel's fingers brushed against the linen napkin as she set her plate down. "We need to pull the right thread to see the whole pattern," she murmured, her detective's intuition stitching together doubt and possibility into a new theory that was just beginning to take shape.

Hazel shuffled forward in the queue, her eyes scanning the spread of breakfast options as she pondered aloud. "But Vivian was boasting about snagging some hot shot vendor for her wool supply," she mused, reaching for a warm muffin and carefully placing it on her plate. "It wasn't Eduardo—she knew she'd lost that deal weeks ago. The contract I saw was dated way before his... incident."

Liam's expression grew pensive as he selected a ripe strawberry from the buffet. "Perhaps whatever fiber was found at the scene might trace back to something in her collection," he suggested, his voice low.

"Even if it does," Hazel replied, scrutinizing a slice of melon with knit brows, "Vivian wouldn't have known the exact weave of the farm's layout, nor how to handle that ornery gate lock." She popped the melon into her mouth, the sweetness of the fruit doing little to temper the bitterness of doubt creeping in.

"Are you second-guessing our statements to the Inspector?" Liam inquired, his gaze fixed on her.

She paused, a half-hearted shrug lifting her shoulders. "I'm not certain Vivian was our culprit," Hazel admitted, her voice tinged with regret. "No motive strong enough to push her to murder Eduardo."

"Then who?" Liam's question hung between them like the steam rising from the hot coffee urn nearby.

"I don't know," she confessed, exhaling a troubled sigh as she picked up a steaming cup of tea. "But it's not Vivian. She's ruthless in business, sure, but killing Eduardo gains her nothing but knots in her already tangled web."

"Indeed, a good point," Liam agreed, a wry smile touching his lips as they both stepped away from the buffet, their plates a colorful collage of the morning's offerings.

Hazel and Liam were nudging their way through the breakfast queue when the man ahead of them, a stout fellow with crumbs already dotting his sweater, swiveled around. His eyes, curious and a touch too eager, met Hazel's. "Excuse me, were you two just talking about Vivian Kensington?"

She nodded, her hand pausing above the tongs meant for the cinnamon rolls. "Yes, that's right. Do you know something about her?"

"Ran into her the other day, we've worked together a few times before," the man said, scratching his chin. "She was bragging about some big deal with a new vendor. Paula, I think? Upscale cashmere dealer."

Liam leaned forward, his brow furrowed in skepticism. "And how do you know this is true?"

"Vivian was standing there, shoulder to shoulder with Paula. They seemed pretty chummy, announcing their partnership to anyone within earshot." He shrugged, as if this sort of gossip was commonplace over scrambled eggs and sausage links.

A heavy sensation settled in Hazel's chest, the kind that came with the unraveling of a carefully knitted theory. She felt her heart drop, the stitches of certainty loosening one by one. The realization hit her: in her desperate attempt not to be deemed a criminal, she may have wrongfully accused Vivian. Her fingers slackened around the tongs, releasing them with a clatter.

"Are you alright, Hazel?" Liam asked, concern lacing his voice as he watched the color drain from her cheeks.

She struggled to swallow past the lump forming in her throat. "I feel dreadful, Liam. I—I might've steered the investigation towards an innocent person." There was a tremor in her voice, a blend of guilt and shock. Despite her personal feelings toward Vivian's dismissive attitude and aggressive business tactics, the notion of her being behind bars for a crime she didn't commit was unsettling.

"An innocent person who didn't deserve this," she murmured, her gaze lost somewhere between the glistening fruit salad and the array of pastries. The evidence they'd supplied the inspectors now appeared as frayed ends of yarn, disconnected from the truth.

"Let's not jump to conclusions just yet," Liam said gently, placing a comforting hand on her shoulder. "We'll figure this out, together."

"Right," Hazel managed a weak smile, the hospitality of the hotel buffet doing little to ease the turmoil within. It was clear they had more sleuthing to do, and time was slipping through their fingers like rogue beads from a broken necklace.

Hazel's fingers hovered over the steaming chafing dishes, but her appetite had vanished like a dropped stitch in one of her intricate cable-knit sweaters. The savory aromas of sizzling bacon and fluffy scrambled eggs filled the air, mingling with the rich scent of freshly brewed coffee, but they did nothing to soothe the knot of anxiety tightening in her gut.

"Hey," she said, turning to Liam, "would you mind if we took our breakfast to go?"

Liam glanced at the laden plates around them, the diners happily chatting as they piled their selections high. He shook his head, his eyes meeting hers with an understanding that went beyond words. "We still have work to do, don't we?" he replied, ever the pragmatist even in the midst of potential culinary delights.

"Quite a bit of it," Hazel confirmed, pushing aside her remorse with a mental shake. "And not a lot of time to untangle this mess."

"Then let's get to it," Liam agreed, his tone light but his gaze resolute.

Together, they passed up on the hotel's breakfast buffet, leaving behind the clinking of cutlery and the hum of early morning conversations. Hazel couldn't help but think of the tangled skeins of yarn back at her shop—how sometimes, you just had to roll up your sleeves and start unraveling.

CHAPTER TWENTY TWO

Hazel popped another egg bite into her mouth, the warmth and savory taste momentarily distracting her from the puzzle at hand. She paced the length of her hotel room, the plush carpet muting her footsteps. Sunlight streamed through the open curtains, casting a soft glow on the assortment of knitting patterns and travel brochures scattered across the bed.

"Where do we even start?" Liam leaned against the mahogany dresser, his arms folded as he watched Hazel's methodical movements. "Especially since we thought we had our culprit and, well, were wrong."

"Give me a break, Liam," Hazel said with a playful roll of her eyes, "this is my first investigation." She stopped pacing and faced him, hands on her hips. "We need to figure out who can get us the information we're missing. That's all."

"Right," Liam nodded, pushing off from the dresser to join in on the brainstorming. "So, we began with the protestors, then Carlos, and finally Vivian."

"Exactly," Hazel affirmed, brushing a loose strand of chestnut hair behind her ear. The protestors had been passionate, their words laced with conviction as they spoke about the anonymous tip regarding Eduardo's alleged cruelty.

"Then we trailed Carlos," Liam continued, recalling the night they followed the man's shadowy figure from the farm to the back alleys of the city. "Only to discover he was channeling funds from Eduardo's farm to pay off his gambling debts."

"And next, we suspected Vivian," Hazel added, the image of the lawyer's file flashing in her mind, the list of rejected proposals stark against the white paper. "Because of how Eduardo was turning down offers left and right."

Liam's gaze met Hazel's, a silent agreement passing between them. They stood side by side in the cozy room, surrounded by the familiar scent of wool and lavender emanating from Hazel's knitting bag. With each revelation, the tangled threads of the mystery seemed to unravel just a little more, guiding them toward the truth they were so determined to uncover.

"Vivian's out of the picture," Liam concluded, his voice carrying a note of certainty. "The gate at the farm was locked from the inside, and she had already secured another supplier. It doesn't add up for her to sabotage Eduardo."

Hazel nodded, her fingers tapping against her chin thoughtfully. "Which means..." She let the sentence hang in the air as if inviting Liam to reach the conclusion with her.

"Carlos?" he ventured, his eyebrows knitting together in contemplation.

"Right. We need to have a chat with Carlos." Hazel's tone was light, but her eyes were sharp with determination. "He might know something about Eduardo selling the farm. Could be a motive tied up somewhere in there."

Liam looked doubtful, running a hand through his tousled hair. "But how do we get him to open up? Last time, he clammed up tighter than a skein of wool."

A mischievous glint appeared in Hazel's eye as she ceased her pacing. She turned to face Liam, a smile playing on her lips. "I have my ways," she said cryptically.

"Uh-oh." Liam's voice carried a playful wariness. "That tone usually means trouble's brewing on the horizon."

"Maybe so, but it's necessary trouble," Hazel assured him, her smile widening. "Besides, we're not going back to the farm."

"Then where?" Liam asked, following Hazel's gaze as she glanced out the window toward the bustling street below.

"We're heading to the bar," she declared, her voice infused with the confidence of someone who'd just solved a particularly tricky cable pattern in their latest knitting project. "Carlos has... habits that make him predictable."

"Ah, the good old watering hole," Liam said, nodding in understanding. "Alright, lead the way, detective."

With a chuckle, Hazel grabbed her bag, slinging it over her shoulder as they made their way out of the hotel room. They stepped into the bright morning sunlight, the anticipation of uncovering new clues infusing their steps with purpose. Together, they headed toward the bar where they hoped to unravel another strand in the mystery of Eduardo's untimely demise.

***

The gravel crunched under the tires of their modest rental car as Hazel and Liam pulled into the parking lot of the run-down bar. It was the sort of place that seemed to soak up the shadows, even under the clear morning sky. Hazel's keen eyes quickly spotted the familiar, battered sedan huddled between two pickup trucks.

"Look," she said, pointing discreetly, "Carlos's chariot awaits."

"Who goes to a bar in the morning?" Liam asked, his brow furrowing as he peered through the windshield at the neon sign flickering half-heartedly above the entrance.

"Probably a guy who's dropping off a payment," Hazel said with a sigh, her voice laced with the frustration of untangling a dropped stitch.

"Right," Liam nodded, the pieces falling into place. "He does still have to pay that off."

They stepped out of the car, the air heavy with the scent of yesterday's stale beer and the unmistakable tang of regret that lingered around places like this. The door of the bar swung open just as they approached, and Carlos emerged, squinting against the brightness of day.

"Hazel?" he scoffed, almost stumbling upon seeing her. "What are you doing here?"

Hazel cocked an eyebrow, her stance casual yet assertive. "Oh, the better question is why you're here, using your father's money to pay for your own gambling debts."

Carlos visibly paled, looking as if he had just snipped the wrong yarn in the middle of a complex knitting project. He took a step back from Hazel, leaning against the sun-bleached siding of the building, the wear and neglect mirroring his expression.

"What—how did you know that?" His voice was barely above a whisper, the bravado of moments ago unraveling rapidly.

Liam watched, impressed by Hazel's knack for pulling at threads until the whole truth came undone. He knew better than to interrupt; after all, watching Hazel work was like observing a master knitter at the loom—a dance of skill and precision that never ceased to amaze him.

Carlos's breath came in a heavy sigh, his eyes shut as if to block out the weight of his predicament. His shoulders sagged, and when they lifted again, there was a reluctant acceptance in his posture. "What is it that you want to know?" he asked, voice resigned.

"We know," Hazel began, her tone firm but not unkind, "and we can either have this conversation between us, or I can walk over to the nearest phone booth and have it with the police instead. Your father's case—well, you being here doesn't cast you in the best light, does it?"

Carlos opened his eyes, just a sliver of defeat showing through as he regarded Hazel. There was no anger in his gaze, only the tired acknowledgment of being cornered. "Did you know about your father's plans to sell part of the farm to developers?" she prodded gently, watching his reaction closely.

His brow furrowed, confusion knitting across his face like misplaced stitches in a carefully planned pattern. "No," Carlos said, shaking his head, his voice a mix of bewilderment and a hint of betrayal. "He never mentioned anything like that."

"Nothing? He didn't discuss it with you before making the decision?" Hazel pressed, trying to untangle the truth.

"No, nothing," Carlos repeated, leaning back against the rough texture of the building. "He loved that land... why would he do that?"

"Supposedly winding down for retirement," Liam chimed in, folding his arms as he studied Carlos. The morning sun caught the lines of concern etched into his features, casting shadows that seemed to deepen with his frown.

"But how could you not know about it?" Hazel's question hung in the air, pointed yet perplexed. "You worked with him. You two were very close"

Carlos appeared to shrink, his hands rubbing up and down his arms in a self-soothing gesture that spoke volumes. "Well, I—" He swallowed hard, as if the confession pained him. "I wasn't exactly involved with the business side of things lately."

Hazel exchanged a glance with Liam, both their expressions full of doubt and curiosity, suspicion weaving through their thoughts. They knew they were close to unraveling the mystery, one loose strand at a time.

Hazel tilted her head, considering the man before her. "So you probably wouldn't know anyone who might be upset about this land sale, someone with a history with the farm?"

"Truthfully?" Carlos's voice had a hollow ring to it, and he shook his head, gaze fixed on some unseen point in the distance. "I didn't even realize the sale was happening. I don't... I haven't been around the farm much." His shoulders slumped, a physical testament to his detachment.

"Has anyone shown an interest in the farm since your father passed?" Liam's question cut through the morning air, straightforward and sharp.

Again, Carlos responded with a negative shake of his head, the motion dislodging a few stray hairs across his forehead. "No clue. I'm not taking over the business."

Hazel blinked, taken aback. "You're not? But you're his son."

Carlos let out a breathy chuckle that lacked any real humor. "Yeah, but... I've always struggled with it, never felt like I could fill his boots." He looked down at his own scuffed shoes, as if they were evidence of his confession. "So I decided to pass it on to my sister."

"Your sister?" Hazel's eyes widened with realization. "I completely forgot Eduardo had another child."

"Lucia," Carlos said, nodding slowly. His posture straightened a bit as he mentioned his sibling's name.

"Lucia..." Hazel repeated, rolling the name around like a new skein of yarn, full of potential. "She might have more insight then. You've been incredibly helpful, Carlos. Thank you." She offered him a small, sympathetic smile. "And, for what it's worth, I think if you got yourself sorted out of this mess," she gestured loosely to their surroundings, "your father would've been proud to see you running the farm."

A brief flash of emotion flickered across Carlos's face, something raw and tender, before he composed himself and gave a mute nod. It was clear he wasn't ready to weave more words into their conversation.

"Thank you, really." Hazel's gratitude was genuine, the warmth in her voice wrapping around Carlos like a well-knit scarf. With a final look, she turned away, her mind already stitching together their next move.

Hazel and Liam left Carlos leaning against the weathered bricks of the bar, his silhouette shrinking in their wake as they walked back to their car. The morning sun cast a warm glow on the dusty parking lot, and the gravel crunched beneath their shoes, punctuating the silence that had settled between them.

"Should we go talk to Lucia now?" Liam asked, squinting against the sunlight, his voice hopeful.

Hazel was about to nod when the cheerful jingle of her phone cut through the air. She fished it from her pocket, eyeing the unknown number before pressing it to her ear.

"Ms. Stitchworth?" came the crisp voice of Inspector Martin, formal as always.

"Speaking," Hazel replied, her eyes narrowing slightly as she braced for news she might not want to hear.

"Could you come into the station to record your statement regarding Vivian's arrest?"

Hazel glanced at Liam, who raised an eyebrow in silent question. "Actually, I'm tied up with a business meeting right now," she lied smoothly, her gaze drifting to the empty lot that certainly didn't resemble anywhere one could grab a bite.

"Is that so?" There was skepticism in Martin's tone, but Hazel wasn't about to let him unravel her alibi.

"Absolutely. And I've got company that you might want to speak with as well," she quipped, gesturing subtly to Liam. "Can he swing by first? He was there for all of this, too."

Inspector Martin let out a resigned sigh. "Fine. But I'll need to speak with you later today, Ms. Stitchworth. If not, I'll have to come find you, and trust me, neither of us wants that."

"Of course, Inspector. No problem at all," Hazel assured him with a smile that carried none of the weight of her words. She ended the call and slipped the phone back into her pocket, feeling the fabric of her jeans brush against her fingertips.

"Looks like you're up, detective," she said, her tone light despite the gravity of their situation. "Seems I've bought us some time, but not much. We need to unravel this before Martin comes knocking with those handcuffs of his."

Liam nodded, the corner of his lips twitching upward. "My heroic sacrifice," he joked, but his eyes were serious. "You better find that missing piece, Hazel."

"Trust me," Hazel said, determination knitting her brows together. "I won't let Vivian rot in there for something she didn't do."

With that, they parted ways, Liam toward the precinct and Hazel with a new destination in mind. As she started the engine, the hum of the car blended with the sounds of the waking town, a soft backdrop to her thoughts as she prepared to meet the enigmatic Lucia.

Hazel pocketed her phone with a deft flick of her wrist, the fabric stretching slightly as she moved. She turned to Liam, who was already eyeing the precinct in the distance with a mix of reluctance and resolve. The early morning sun glinted off the windows, giving the building an almost welcoming gleam that belied the tension simmering between them.

"Lucia might be our golden ticket, Liam," Hazel said, optimism threading through her words like a silver strand in a tapestry of doubt.

"She could have the clue we're missing, the one that points to who's really behind this whole tangled mess."

Liam, leaning against their car, crossed his arms and raised an eyebrow. "Yeah, but while you're out there playing master detective, I'm stuck giving a statement I'd rather stitch my mouth shut than deliver."

"Aw, come on, it's not so bad," Hazel replied, her voice a soft chide as she nudged him playfully with her elbow. "You'll be back in the fray before you know it. Just buy me some time, stall for about thirty minutes or so. That should be enough for me to get the name we need."

"Stall?" Liam echoed, his tone halfway between amusement and exasperation. "What do you expect me to do? Knit Inspector Martin a scarf?"

"Ha! If only you could." Hazel chuckled, the sound bubbling up from deep within her like a brook over smooth stones. "Just keep him busy. You're good with yarns—stories, I mean. Spin him one."

"Fine, fine," Liam conceded, shaking his head with a reluctant grin tugging at his lips. "But just remember, you owe me one—and I'm not talking about a knitted beanie."

"Promise," Hazel said, her nod firm, sealing the deal like a knot at the end of a thread. She watched Liam saunter away, his steps measured and purposeful, before turning on her heel and heading toward her own destination.

With every step Hazel took, the sounds of the town wrapped around her—the distant murmur of conversations from nearby shops, the rhythmic clack of shoes on pavement, the occasional car engine rumbling past. It all blended into a familiar melody, one that spoke of home and comfort, even as her mind raced with the urgency of the investigation.

She didn't know what awaited her when she would meet Lucia, but Hazel Stitchworth never backed down from a challenge, whether it was unraveling a complex knitting pattern or weaving together the loose threads of a mystery. And with each stride, she was one step closer to pulling the right string that would unravel the truth.

CHAPTER TWENTY THREE

Hazel maneuvered the borrowed sedan up the familiar gravel path of Eduardo's farm, her hands gripping the steering wheel with a practiced ease. She was glad that they had time to switch out cars, because she was much more comfortable driving this one around. And now she could come and go as she pleased, as could Liam.

As she rounded the final bend, the farmhouse came into view, and so did an unfamiliar vehicle parked somewhat haphazardly in the driveway. "Well, that must be Lucia's ride," Hazel muttered to herself, her curious gaze tracing the sleek lines of the car.

With a soft sigh, she killed the engine and stepped out into the warm embrace of the countryside air, rich with the earthy scent of hay and the distant bleating of sheep. As her feet crunched on the gravel, she retrieved her phone from the pocket of her cardigan—a hand-knit number featuring an intricate lattice pattern—and quickly typed out a message to Liam.

"Made it to the farm. About to get the name. Keep Inspector Martin on standby." She hit send, and within moments, her screen lit up with Liam's response.

"Okay, going in to interrogation now. Be careful."

Hazel couldn't help but smile at his concern. "Always am," she replied before slipping the phone back into her pocket. The farm felt different without Liam's tall, reassuring presence beside her. But then again, she thought wryly, she had faced down more tangled yarn disasters than she could count; a little solo sleuthing was nothing new.

As she approached the cluster of wooden pens and barns, Hazel's attention was drawn to a figure beyond the enclosures. A younger woman, hair pulled back in a practical ponytail, stood absorbed in her task amidst the rustic setting of the small barn.

"Lucia?" Hazel called out, her tone friendly yet carrying enough to bridge the distance.

The woman turned, her expression guarded as she laid down a pair of well-worn gardening gloves. "Yes, how can I help you?" Her voice was cautious but not unfriendly, much like the wary stance of the farm animals eying Hazel from their pens.

"I was a friend of your father's," Hazel began, her words gentle, as if weaving comfort into the very fabric of the conversation. "Just wanted to see how you were holding up."

"About as well as can be," Lucia replied, the corners of her mouth lifting ever so slightly in a weary semblance of a smile.

"Understandable," Hazel nodded, her eyes taking in the details of Lucia's weathered barn jacket and the faint traces of soil under her fingernails—signs of hard work and dedication. It was clear Lucia was no stranger to the ebb and flow of farm life, and something about her reminded Hazel of a stubborn knot that required patience and a deft touch to untangle.

Hazel stepped into the sun-drenched opening of the barn, her eyes adjusting to the contrast between the bright outdoors and the shady interior. The scent of hay and earth filled the air, a familiar fragrance that reminded her of childhood visits to her aunt's farm.

"Nobody could ever prepare themselves for such a loss," Hazel said, the warmth in her voice wrapping around Lucia like a soft, hand-knitted shawl. "I'm really sorry."

Lucia offered a small smile, one that didn't quite reach her eyes but was genuine all the same. "It's tough, losing Dad," she admitted, tucking a stray lock of hair behind her ear. "But I feel him around, you know? In the rustle of the leaves and the creak of the barn door. It's... comforting."

"That's really sweet," Hazel replied, her heart twining with empathy for the young woman before her. "Of course, he's there for you." She took a step closer, her own hands itching for the comfort of her knitting needles—there was something about the repetitive motion that soothed the soul. "I was hoping to ask you a few questions if that's okay?"

"Of course," Lucia said, brushing the dirt from her hands onto her jeans. "Feel free."

"Did you know much about what your brother, Carlos, has been up to?" Hazel ventured, observing Lucia's face for any flicker of emotion.

Lucia let out a sigh, the weight of concern etched into the lines of her forehead. "Yes, I've noticed he's been... less present lately." Her gaze drifted off to a corner of the barn where tools were neatly arranged, each in its proper place. "That's why I've had to step in more. I knew he couldn't juggle it all."

"Juggling can be tricky unless you have the right pattern to follow," Hazel quipped, an attempt to lighten the moment with her characteristic humor. "And speaking of patterns, did you know about his gambling?"

There was a brief pause, a moment of quiet where even the barn seemed to hold its breath. Lucia's nod was slow, almost reluctant. "He's always had a problem with it," she finally said, her voice tinged with sadness. "Gambling can unravel the best of us. But I'm hoping he seeks the help he needs soon."

Hazel leaned against the rough wooden frame of the barn door, taking in the earthy scent of hay and the faint clucking of chickens from a nearby coop. She watched Lucia, noticing the way her hands never stopped moving, tidying tools as she spoke.

"Lucia," Hazel ventured with a casual tilt of her head, "did your father have issues with anyone before...?" She trailed off delicately, a skill she'd honed like the fine point of her favorite knitting needle.

Lucia brushed a strand of hair from her face, stained with the effort of farm work. "Well, I'm not entirely certain," she began, pausing to consider her words. "But after he sold that big portion of the land, it seemed like he was turning people away more frequently."

"Right," Hazel murmured, her response automatic as her mind knitted together the strands of information. But how did Lucia come by this knowledge? Was it common gossip, or had she read it somewhere, woven into the threads of the internet?

The question itched at Hazel like a wool sweater on bare skin, and she couldn't help but pull at the loose yarn. "Speaking of the property sale..." Hazel approached the subject as she would a delicate lace pattern, with care and precision. "Did he ever share with you why he decided to sell?"

Lucia paused, her gaze landing on a pitchfork leaning against the barn wall. "Oh, yes," she responded, a bit too quickly for Hazel's liking. "He mentioned looking to buy property elsewhere."

A chill ran down Hazel's spine, as unsettling as dropping a stitch in the middle of a complicated cable pattern. If Lucia had stumbled upon the story of the land sale online, surely she would have also seen Eduardo's reasons for selling - to retire and downsize, not to reinvest.

"Interesting," Hazel said, her voice light but her mind racing. Her intuition, honed by hours of patient knitting, told her something about Lucia's pattern didn't quite match up. The pieces were there, but they weren't fitting together seamlessly. And in both knitting and sleuthing, Hazel knew the importance of unraveling a mystery until every thread fell into place.

"Great, well, one moment," Hazel said, her fingers deftly pulling out her phone as if she were selecting the perfect needle for a new knitting project. Thumbs dancing over the screen, she sent a quick text—911—to Liam, the wordless signal they'd agreed upon for urgent situations. Her thumbs hovered above the keyboard to weave an explanation when Lucia's voice broke her concentration.

"Is everything alright?" Lucia's inquiry held a note of genuine concern—or was it a touch of suspicion?

"Yep, just have the information I need," Hazel replied with a practiced ease, sliding her phone back into her pocket like a trusty stitch marker safely tucked away until needed again. She could feel Lucia's gaze on her, inquisitive and searching.

"Are you sure you've got everything you need?" Lucia pressed, her eyes narrowing ever so slightly, as though trying to read the pattern of Hazel's intentions.

Hazel nodded, her face betraying none of the unease that knit together her thoughts. "I'm just going to leave now."

As Hazel turned to go, she caught the subtle shift in Lucia's expression; it was like watching a dropped stitch unravel a row of careful work. "Are you actually some kind of cop or reporter?" Lucia asked, her words laced with a hint of accusation.

"No, nothing of the sort," Hazel assured her, shaking her head with the same rhythm she'd shake out a skein of yarn before winding it. She paused, a notion catching in her mind like a snag in fine lace. "I'm guessing," she ventured carefully, "that you didn't know your father was planning to slow down before retirement?"

Lucia remained silent, her lips pinched into a tight line, twisting to the side as if to avoid snagging on the truth. It was a tell-tale sign, one that Hazel, always attuned to the subtleties of body language as much as the tension of yarn, couldn't overlook.

The air in the barn seemed to still, heavy with the scent of hay and the unspoken thoughts hanging between them. Hazel waited for a moment longer, allowing the silence to stretch like a pause between rows on a knitting chart. Then, without another word, she turned on her heel and walked towards her car, leaving behind the silence and the barn with its secrets nestled within.

Hazel stepped closer, her shadow merging with Lucia's on the dust-flecked barn floor. The afternoon sun cast a soft light through the open doors, illuminating the straw-littered space and the tension that wrapped around them like yarn too tightly wound.

"Lucia," Hazel started, her voice even but carrying the weight of her suspicions, "you're familiar with every nook of this land, aren't you? The gate that's always sticking, the fences that need mending." She gestured toward the expanse beyond the barn, where the property stretched out like a green quilt waiting to be stitched together. "You'd have more of it all – more land, more business, more money – if you were in charge, without your father selling off pieces."

Lucia's eyes flickered, the only movement in her otherwise statuesque pose. She was as still as a skein of wool before it's touched by knitting needles.

"Tell me I'm wrong," Hazel pressed on, her heart beating a staccato rhythm akin to the click-clack of bamboo knitting needles at work. "Tell me you didn't kill your own father."

The accusation hung between them, floating like down feathers escaped from a farmhand's pillow. Lucia's expression shifted, the corners of her mouth twitching as if she were trying to knit her features into a pattern of innocence. But the design was flawed, the outcome unclear.

CHAPTER TWENTY FOUR

The unsettling timbre of Lucia's laughter wove through the stillness of the evening air, a sinister melody that clung to Hazel's skin like dew on morning grass. It was a laugh devoid of warmth, one that carried the weight of secrets too long kept hidden.

"Alright," Lucia conceded with a theatrical sigh, as if she were unraveling the climax of a mystery novel rather than confessing to patricide. "I suppose I can come clean—it's just us here, after all." She leaned in closer, her breath tickling Hazel's ear. "Yes, I killed him. Stabbed him with a shearing knife, straight to the back. Poor Daddy never saw it coming."

Hazel fought to keep her composure, her fingers itching for the comfort of knitting needles, something familiar and grounding. Instead, she found herself untangling this most macabre yarn. "Was it for the business?" she ventured, voice steady despite the tremors that threatened to betray her. "For the land?"

Lucia's nod came with a self-satisfied smile, as though she were admiring a perfectly executed cable knit. "Oh, yes. I couldn't let the business sit and rot in his hands—he wanted to downsize. Can you imagine? We could've had it all. There was this whole property and I have plans for every inch of it. My dad wasn't able to see the potential this place had. He stuck with his small time shop, but I wanted an empire. And my brother..." Her lips curled around the word, an imperfect stitch in her otherwise seamless facade. "A disappointment, just like our father. I'm the one who will make it perfect. I'm here now to make sure this place gets me the money I deserve."

As if to punctuate her declaration, Lucia's hand emerged from the folds of her cardigan, glinting metal catching the last rays of the setting sun. The shearing scissors loomed large in Hazel's vision, an ominous echo of the weapon of choice that had ended Eduardo's life.

"Well, that's one way to cut ties," quipped Hazel, unable to suppress her instinctive humor even as her mind raced for a solution that didn't end with her name etched on a tombstone. After all, she mused grimly, there were better ways to sever relationships than with literal shears.

Hazel's eyes widened as the shearing scissors glinted menacingly in Lucia's grip. She could almost hear her grandmother's voice in her head, chiding her for not being more alert to the looming danger—like a dropped stitch about to unravel an entire sweater.

"Lucia, you don't need to do this," Hazel pleaded, taking cautious steps backward, her hands raised in a gesture of peace—or perhaps, in the hopes of knitting together a truce.

But Lucia's resolve was knotted tightly with ambition. "But I do," she hissed, stepping forward with the confidence of someone who had just finished the perfect skein of yarn. "I'm not going to lose everything now that I finally have it." Her voice carried a chilling finality that echoed against the vast expanse of land around them.

With no time to spare for another word, Hazel spun on her heel and bolted across the field. The soft earth gave way beneath her feet, her shoes kicking up clods of dirt as she raced toward the copse of trees at the far end of the property. They seemed so distant, like a safe harbor bobbing on the horizon of a stormy sea.

Behind her, the sound of Lucia's pursuit was a cacophony that drowned out all other thought. Every gasp of breath, every pounding heartbeat was a drumbeat urging her to move faster. Don't look back, she commanded herself, remembering the countless times she'd fumbled her knitting by losing focus. This was one pattern she couldn't afford to drop.

The first trees of the sanctuary loomed ahead, their bark rough under her fingers as she darted into their embrace. She wove between the trunks with the agility of someone threading a needle in haste, leaving no straight path for Lucia to follow. The world became a blur of green and brown, the rustle of leaves above whispering secrets of escape.

Finally, the footsteps behind her began to fade, slowing like the tension easing from a too-tight yarn ball. Hazel allowed herself to slow as well, each step more deliberate until she came to a standstill behind the broad trunk of an ancient oak. Its rough bark pressed into her back, a solid presence in a moment fraught with uncertainty.

Catching her breath, Hazel listened intently, hoping her own racing pulse wouldn't betray her hiding spot. For now, she had evaded Lucia's sharp edges, but the next part of her escape was yet to be knit together.

Hazel's lungs burned like the hot sun, her breaths coming out in ragged stitches. She huddled behind the oak, its ancient bark pressing into her spine like the blunt end of a knitting needle. Her fingers trembled, not from crafting a delicate lace pattern, but from gripping her phone so tightly it might as well have been yarn wound too close to snapping.

It was hard to keep completely silent. In fact, she felt like every breath, every movement was enough to alert the killer to her position. Still, she knew she needed to do something, anything productive to give herself a sliver of hope.

She pull out her phone from her pocket slowly. She was about to send another SOS to Liam when Lucia's voice shattered the fragile silence. "Hazel, come out, come out wherever you are!" The sing-song menace of her taunt knitted a cold pattern down Hazel's back.

Frozen, Hazel didn't dare even to blink, hoping her stillness would render her invisible. Slowly, she slid her phone back into her pocket, unable to risk the sound of her tapping. But the false security unraveled with a small betrayal—a stick beneath her sneaker snapped like a weak link in a chain stitch. Panic needled her as she cursed her clumsy foot and bolted.

Think, think, she urged herself. If she could just reach the neighbors...

Her flight was a mad dash of desperation, legs pumping with the kind of energy usually reserved for last-minute holiday knitting marathons. The idea of sanctuary spurred her on until the cruel glint of barb wire loomed ahead, strung tight like a row of purl stitches no one could hope to slip past.

"Of all the fences to run into, it had to be barb wire," Hazel muttered, skidding to a halt. She eyed the menacing tangles, knew there'd be no gentle unraveling from that snare. It wasn't just the barbs either, in a life or death situation, Hazel would have gladly chosen bleeding over dead. But the wires weren't strong enough to hold her and the fence was too tall to climb over with stepping on them. She would tangle herself in the lines and would become only an easier target for Lucia.

Turning back toward the house meant facing Lucia's sharp shears, but staying put was akin to waiting for the scissors to snip her final thread. Choices dwindled like yarn balls worn down to their last few loops, leaving Hazel with little to knit together in terms of a plan.

Hazel's breath came in ragged stitches, each one a frayed edge of fear as she turned to face the grim reality of her potential fate. Lucia loomed before her, the shearing scissors glinting ominously in the dying light, her chest heaving from the exertion of the chase.

"You're out of time, Hazel," Lucia panted, a wild look in her eyes that sent an icy dread through Hazel's veins. It was the same chilling expression she imagined Eduardo had seen in his final moments.

A flash of terror knotted in Hazel's stomach. Was this how her story would be clipped short? But then, piercing through the terrifying hush of the standoff, voices carried on the wind—strong, determined, closing in fast.

"Stop! Police!" Inspector Martin's authoritative shout broke through the tense air. Relief flooded Hazel's senses like warm wool on a cold night.

Lucia's head whipped around, her scissor-wielding hand faltering as she caught sight of Inspector Martin advancing with his gun raised. "Drop the weapon!" he bellowed, every ounce of his command aimed squarely at Lucia.

It was then that Liam burst onto the scene, his face etched with concern. He sprinted towards Hazel and enveloped her in an embrace that felt like a fortress against the chaos. "I was so worried about you," he exhaled, his voice thick with emotion. "Are you okay?"

Hazel nodded against his chest, her heart still racing but slowly untangling from the grip of panic. "I'm okay now," she managed to say, her words weaving into the safety of his hold.

The click of metal hitting the ground punctuated the moment as Lucia dropped her sheers, her hands lifting in defeat. Her face twisted into a snarl, the rage of a plan unraveled written across her features.

"Hands up!" Inspector Martin repeated, moving closer as Lia and Hazel separated, their gazes locked on the woman who'd almost cut the pattern of their lives short.

The crunch of gravel underfoot punctuated the tense silence as they made their way back to the old stone house that had seen better days. The evening sun cast long shadows across the yard, making the scene appear almost picturesque if not for the somber procession leading a handcuffed Lucia to Inspector Martin's squad car.

"Alright, Hazel," Inspector Martin said, his voice firm but not unkind, as he shut the door on Lucia and turned to face her. "I need you to run it by me once more. How did you piece it all together?"

Hazel took a deep breath, still trying to steady her nerves, and managed a small smile. "Lucia slipped up when she told me why Eduardo was selling the property. It didn't add up," she began, her fingers absently playing with the yarn bracelet around her wrist. "She would've only known about the transfer papers if she'd been snooping—she wanted to keep tabs on the company, her eyes on the prize."

"Go on," urged Inspector Martin, leaning against the hood of the car, his attention fixed on her.

"Her ambition blinded her to reason. It was...it was blind rage," Hazel continued, her gaze drifting towards the fading light. "And the lock? Well, who else knew it as intimately as family?"

"Then there's the fabric." Hazel paused, a shiver running through her despite the warmth of the evening. "It should match one of Lucia's shirts. If I know my threads—and I do—that's the final knot in this twisted skein."

Inspector Martin nodded, his eyes softening with relief. "Well, we may have followed the wrong pattern at first, but we got there in the end. Thanks to you."

Lucia's voice, tainted with resignation yet laced with sarcasm, broke through from the backseat of the car. "Just make sure Vivian and I are cleared of our charges, then I guess we're square."

"Of course, you're cleared," Inspector Martin replied, his tone official now. He looked over at Hazel, a hint of a smile playing on his lips. "It was quite the collaboration, though I can't say it was a pleasure, Lucia."

"Hey," Lucia called out, her voice muffled by the car window, "you might want to thank your boyfriend. He's the one who tipped us off."

Inspector Martin chuckled, glancing at Liam who stood a few paces away, his concern for Hazel evident in his posture. "Seems like you owe him one."

Hazel rolled her eyes, a mix of embarrassment and gratitude coloring her cheeks. "My hero," she quipped, looking at Liam with a teasing glint in her eye. "Guess every mystery needs a knight in shining... denim?"

They laughed, a release of tension rippling through them. As the laughter subsided, Hazel gazed at the house, its windows catching the last rays of sunlight, turning them into glowing orbs. Despite everything, it felt good to be standing here, unraveling the truth with threads of justice, her hands finally still.

As Inspector Martin's feet stepped on the path leading to his squad car, Hazel opened her mouth to set the record straight about Liam. But before she could weave a single word into the conversation, the car door closed with a thud, and the inspector drove off, leaving behind a cloud of dust and assumptions.

Hazel turned to Liam, the dusky pink sky softening the edges of the day's harrowing events. "But seriously," she spoke earnestly, a small smile tugging at her lips despite the chaos they'd just untangled. "You really did save me, not just back there but throughout this whole thing."

Liam's gaze held warmth as he brushed a strand of hair that had escaped her ponytail during the chase. "It was the 911 text that saved you," he corrected gently, his voice steady as the loom of a trusty knitting machine. "And everything else... because I wanted to help you. You're a good person, Hazel."

"Thank you," she murmured, feeling the sincerity in his words wrap around her like a hand-knitted shawl on a chilly evening.

The air around them hummed with a newfound stillness, the earlier adrenaline rush now giving way to tranquility. "What's next?" Liam inquired, his eyes searching hers for clues.

Hazel glanced at her watch, its hands ticking away the moments with relentless precision. "I have about ten hours before I need to be on a flight, so packing up and leaving, I guess." Her voice wavered slightly, the thought of departure weaving a twinge of sadness through her heartstrings.

"Then to the hotel," Liam declared, extending his arm with a chivalrous flourish that seemed to mock their earlier peril.

Hazel looped her arm through his, her chuckle mingling with the rustling leaves above them. "To the hotel," she echoed, allowing herself to lean into the comfort of his presence. As they strolled towards the inn, the sunset painted the sky in shades of closure and new beginnings, the stitches of their shared experience forming a pattern neither of them had anticipated.

CHAPTER TWENTY FIVE

Hazel's foot beat a soft rhythm against the marble floor of the hotel lobby, an unconscious testament to the whirlwind of nerves and relief that spun through her. Her fingers wrapped around the handle of her suitcase, the click-clack of luxury luggage wheels a soothing counterpoint to her heartbeat. The last few days had felt like a tangled mess, but now, with answers fitting securely back into her life, she could finally exhale.

"Prison garb is so not your color," Rosemary had teased on the phone, voice thick with unshed tears and the warmth that only an older sister could weave into words. Fiona, ever the pillar of strength, had offered a virtual hug through the phone line, her practicality a balm to Hazel's frayed emotions.

As she walked through the lobby, Hazel thought about the woman on the plane. The one who clearly didn't want to talk to her about her fiber festival, or her yarn, or her store. It seemed funny now that the one thing that made her seem odd, helped Hazel solve the crime. She needed these skills, this passion, to bring justice to a friend and clear her name. She smiled at the thought of proving to that woman that her passion wasn't weird or unremarkable, but something great.

Amidst the lingering scent of polished wood and fresh flowers, the elevator emitted a cheerful ding, pulling Hazel from her thoughts. She looked up, expecting to see Liam's familiar grin walk out and eyes that held deep hues of the ocean. Instead, Vivian Kensington emerged, the queen of mass-produced yarns, her suitcases gliding like sleek merino threads across the floor.

Hazel's breath hitched, caught in the delicate lacework of guilt and surprise. She'd been wrong about Vivian, as wrong as a dropped stitch in a complex Aran pattern. The woman stood before her, an elegant figure amidst the grandeur of the lobby, her silence hanging between them like an unfinished row waiting to be purled.

"Vivian, I..." Hazel started, the apology coiling in her chest, ready to be unraveled. "I'm truly sorry for what happened. For suspecting you... for everything."

The words felt clumsy, like knitting with needles far too large for the yarn, but they were sincere. Hazel held Vivian's gaze, the weight of her remorse as tangible as the hand-spun fibers that she so cherished. This was a tangle she was determined to smooth out, one heartfelt strand at a time.

Vivian's arms folded across her chest like a shawl wrapped tight against a chill, creating a barrier as clear as the invisible walls of her cell had been. "It was really horrible. I couldn't believe you did that. But, I guess, at least you got me out too," she said, her voice carrying the slight tremor of unraveled nerves.

"Right," Hazel agreed, warmth returning to her voice despite the awkwardness that clung to them like lint on a freshly knitted sweater. "I'm so glad they found out who really murdered Eduardo."

A faint sigh escaped Vivian's lips, her disappointment knitting together her finely arched brows. "I was really disappointed that you thought I was actually capable of murder."

Hazel nodded, acknowledging the dropped stitch in her judgment. "I know, it was a stretch. I shouldn't have knit together a case without proper evidence. I'm sorry."

"Apology accepted," Vivian conceded after a moment stretched taut as a skein of yarn. The words seemed to weave a fragile peace between them, but the silence that followed hung heavily, like dense wool fogging up a clear window.

Vivian finally turned on her heel, her departure as sleek and smooth as the silk blends she peddled. Hazel watched her go, then turned her attention to the front desk where another pair of familiar faces were wrapping up their check-out process. Georgia and Leonard looked as though someone had snipped the joy right out of their day, leaving frayed edges in its place.

"Georgia, Leonard," Hazel greeted them, her voice soft but steady.

They turned, expressions as droopy as unblocked lace.

"Of course, I forgive you both," Hazel said, her tone earnest as a promise stitch. "Just, from now on, maybe choose your friendships over business deals?"

Leonard's adam's apple bobbed like a bobbin in his throat as he swallowed hard. Georgia nodded, her reply coming out in a rush. "Of course, always. It shouldn't have even been a question."

"Alright then," Hazel offered them a small smile, the kind that could mend rifts in any social fabric. "See you at the next one?"

"See you at the next one," Leonard echoed, a hint of the old warmth returning to his voice.

Hazel's gaze was fixed on the ornate grandfather clock across the hotel lobby, its pendulum swinging with a rhythm more calming than the clicking of her knitting needles. The hands inched forward, marking the passing minutes with a pace that felt too sluggish considering the week she'd had. Suddenly, her phone erupted with a jarring ring, slicing through the quiet hum of the lobby.

She glanced down, and for a split second, her heart stalled. Eduardo's name flashed on the screen, a reminder of the man who would never call again. With a steadying breath, she answered, “Hello?”

"Uh, hi. Hazel? It's Carlos," came the apologetic voice from the other end. "Sorry to use this number—I didn’t have any other way to reach you."

"Carlos, it's alright," Hazel assured him, a pang of sympathy threading through her words. "What's going on?"

"Well," he began, his voice fraught with the weight of his decision, "I heard about my sister's arrest. I've been thinking a lot about what you said, and I've decided to take over for my father."

"Wow, that's fantastic, Carlos," Hazel exclaimed, her relief knitting itself into a smile. "Good for you."

"Thanks," he replied, the sound of his resolve evident even through the phone. "I'm going ahead with the sale of the property—to pay off the debts, get clean, and keep running the farm. Like Dad would’ve wanted."

"That's great news," Hazel said, genuine warmth woven into her words. "You deserve a good life, Carlos. And Eduardo... he would have definitely wanted that for you."

"Means a lot to hear you say that," Carlos admitted. "I’ll give you a call within the next week to send your order over."

"Fantastic," Hazel chuckled, her spirits lifting at the promise of returning to familiar routines. "Can't wait."

"Alright, I'll talk to you soon. Got a few things to sort out first."

"Good luck with everything, Carlos." Hazel pressed the phone closer, as if the sincerity of her well-wishes could travel through the signal.

"Thanks, Hazel. Bye for now."

"Bye, Carlos." She hung up, the corners of her mouth curling upwards in a hopeful grin.

Tucking her phone into her pocket, the soft chime of the elevator bell echoed through the space. It heralded another departure, another shift in the intricate pattern of her life. Hazel felt a thread of anticipation weave through her core. She was ready to cast off from this tangled skein of events and start fresh back home.

The metallic chime signaled Liam's arrival, and Hazel swiveled on her heel, the soft click of her shoes muted against the plush carpet of the hotel lobby. Her eyes found his, and a reciprocal smile played on their lips as they closed the distance between them, their steps syncing in an unspoken rhythm.

"Can't imagine what this week would've been like without you," she said, tucking a stray lock of hair behind her ear. "I'd probably be mastering the art of knitting with toothbrushes behind bars by now."

Liam's chuckle was a low rumble, a comforting sound that seemed to wrap around her like a warm shawl. "And I'd have had a very boring week," he replied, shrugging off the gravity of her words with an ease that only made him more endearing. "Plus, I'd have missed out on something quite remarkable."

Her cheeks felt suddenly warm, and Hazel tilted her head down for a moment, pretending to adjust the handle on her suitcase. The budding connection between them was as delicate and intricate as lacework, and she wasn't quite ready to hold it up to the light just yet.

"Airport?" she suggested, nodding towards the revolving doors that marked the threshold between their current adventure and the world beyond.

"Absolutely," Liam agreed, but then paused, his gaze holding hers with gentle intensity. "Just promise me one thing?"

"Anything," she responded, her heart doing a little stitch-and-purl at the earnest look in his eyes.

"Keep in touch. Once we part ways at the airport, I don't want our story to end on the last page of this chapter."

Hazel's smile spread slowly, as if each word from Liam was another row added to a pattern she was eager to see completed. "I will. I mean—after all the threads we've untangled together, how could I not?"

They wheeled their suitcases side by side, leaving the cocoon of the hotel's lobby for the brisk air outside, where the weave of passing cars and bustling people reminded them of the world waiting to be stitched back into their lives.

Hazel gave a firm nod, her fingers interlacing around the leather strap of her suitcase. "Absolutely," she echoed with a promise stitched into her voice.

Liam's shoulders relaxed, a satisfied grin playing at the corners of his mouth. "Good," he said, rolling his suitcase with a clack-clack rhythm over the marbled floor of the hotel lobby. "I'm ready to leave this country and get back home where I can just relax."

The sound of their laughter mingled with the soft hum of conversation around them. Hazel chuckled, her eyes twinkling with the shared memory of chaos and close calls. "Yeah, until the next one," she replied, the hint of adventure already lacing her words.

Liam cast a sideways glance at her, his hand running through his hair—a gesture she'd come to recognize as his contemplation sign. "But the next one won't be as stressful as this one, will it?" he asked, half-hoping, half-teasing.

She shrugged, her lips curving into a smile that held both wisdom and whimsy. "You never know," Hazel quipped, her gaze lifting to meet his.

Her response hung in the air between them, a playful challenge, an invitation to future escapades. It was a sentiment as comforting as the knit pashmina she wore around her shoulders—soft, warm, and full of potential patterns yet to emerge.

They continued toward the sliding glass doors that whispered open, ushering them towards new horizons. The sun outside cast a gentle glow on the world, wrapping the end of their current mystery in a golden light, leaving them to wonder what the next chapter might hold.

NOW AVAILABLE!

WOOLEN WITNESS
(A Hazel Stitchworth Cozy Mystery—Book 2)

"A great story of murder, romance, new beginnings, love, friendships and a wonderful cascade of mystery."
--Amazon reviewer (regarding *Murder in the Manor*)

WOOLEN WITNESS: A HAZEL STITCHWORTH COZY MYSTERY (BOOK #2) is the second book in a new cozy mystery series by Fiona Grace, #1 bestselling author of *Murder in the Manor*, which has over 10,000 five star reviews!

When knitter and boutique owner Hazel Stitchworth heads to Scotland for an elite knitting convention, things quickly spirals from stitch to hitch when her icon is killed amidst the revelry, leaving behind an unfinished pattern that could lead to the killer.

Can Hazel and her new beau Liam knit the loose ends together? Or will the murderer slip through her fingers like so many silken threads?

Immerse yourself in the enchanting world of the Hazel Stitchworth series, a warm and inviting cozy mystery that seamlessly blends sharp wit and peculiar charm. With its blend of lighthearted comedy, heartfelt emotions, and unexpected plot turns, this series is sure to present an endearing new protagonist who will steal your heart and keep you engrossed until the early morning hours.

Future books in the series are also available!

"Very entertaining. I highly recommend this book to the permanent library of any reader that appreciates a very well written mystery, with some twists and an intelligent plot. You will not be disappointed. Excellent way to spend a cold weekend!"
--Books and Movie Reviews, Roberto Mattos (regarding *Murder in the Manor*)

"The story line wasn't just a who done it, but had a story about her life and romance, including village life. Very entertaining."
--Amazon reviewer (regarding *Murder in the Manor*)

"It has endearing and sometimes quirky characters, a plot that keeps you reading and the right amount of romance. I can't wait to start book two!"
--Amazon reviewer (regarding *Murder in the Manor*)

"What a great story of murder, romance, new beginnings, love, friendships and a wonderful cascade of mystery."
--Amazon reviewer (regarding *Murder in the Manor*)

"This is a clean contemporary romance that you will find hard to put down!"
--Amazon reviewer (regarding *Always, Forever*)

"A bit of romance and a very determined woman! I have read many of Fiona Grace's novels and loved every one of them—this was no exception. I am looking forward to reading the rest of this new series!"
--Amazon reviewer (regarding *Always, With You*)

Fiona Grace

Fiona Grace is author of the LACEY DOYLE COZY MYSTERY series, comprising nine books; of the TUSCAN VINEYARD COZY MYSTERY series, comprising seven books; of the DUBIOUS WITCH COZY MYSTERY series, comprising three books; of the BEACHFRONT BAKERY COZY MYSTERY series, comprising six books; of the CATS AND DOGS COZY MYSTERY series, comprising nine books; of the ELIZA MONTAGU COZY MYSTERY series, comprising nine books (and counting); of the ENDLESS HARBOR ROMANTIC COMEDY series, comprising nine books (and counting); of the INN AT DUNE ISLAND ROMANTIC COMEDY series, comprising seven books (and counting); of the INN BY THE SEA ROMANTIC COMEDY series, comprising five books (and counting); of the MAID AND THE MANSION COZY MYSTERY series, comprising five books (and counting); of the ALICE BLOOM COZY MYSTERY series, comprising five books (and counting); of the MAGNOLIA BAY COZY MYSTERY series, comprising five books (and counting); of the TIMBERLAKE TITANS HOCKEY ROMANCE series, comprising five books (and counting); of the ASHVILLE ACES HOCKEY ROMANCE series, comprising five books (and counting); of the PENNY HAWTHORNE cozy mystery series, comprising seven books (and counting); and of the DELILAH GREEN cozy mystery series, comprising five books (and counting).

Fiona would love to hear from you, so please visit www.fionagraceauthor.com to receive free ebooks, hear the latest news, and stay in touch.

BOOKS BY FIONA GRACE

DELILAH GREEN COZY MYSTERY
ORCHID OBSESSION (Book #1)
LETHAL LEAVES (Book #2)
BETRAYAL IN BLOOM (Book #3)
SINISTER SEEDS (Book #4)
FATAL FOLIAGE (Book #5)

PENNY HAWTHORNE COZY MYSTERY
HERBAL HOMICIDE (Book #1)
VANILLA VENDETTA (Book #2)
PEPPERMINT PERIL (Book #3)
MINTY MALICE (Book #4)
CHAMOMILE CALAMITY (Book #5)
FENNEL FATALITY (Book #6)
EARL GREY ALIBI (Book #7)

ASHVILLE ACES HOCKEY ROMANCE
BREAKAWAY BLISS (Book #1)
ICY INTIMACY (Book #2)
FACEOFF FLING (Book #3)
RINK RENDEZVOUS (Book #4)
HOCKEY HEARTTHROB (Book #5)

TIMBERLAKE TITANS HOCKEY ROMANCE
RINKSIDE ROMANCE (Book #1)
FLIRTY FACEOFF (Book #2)
MELTING THE ICE (Book #3)
THE PUCK STOPS HERE (Book #4)
GLOVES DROP, LOVE BLOOMS (Book #5)

MAGNOLIA BAY COZY MYSTERY
THE TAINTED TAFFY (Book #1)
A MASKED MURDER (Book #2)
A CAFE CONFESSION (Book #3)
THE FROZEN FIND (Book #4)
A CURIOUS CURSE (Book #5)

THE MAID AND THE MANSION COZY MYSTERY

A MYSTERIOUS MURDER (Book #1)

A SCANDALOUS DEATH (Book #2)

A MISSING GUEST (Book #3)

AN UNSOLVABLE CRIME (Book #4)

AN IMPOSSIBLE HEIST (Book #5)

INN BY THE SEA ROMANTIC COMEDY

A NEW LOVE (Book #1)

A NEW CHANCE (Book #2)

A NEW HOME (Book #3)

A NEW LIFE (Book #4)

A NEW ME (Book #5)

THE INN AT DUNE ISLAND ROMANTIC COMEDY

A CHANCE LOVE (Book #1)

A CHANCE FALL (Book #2)

A CHANCE ROMANCE (Book #3)

A CHANCE CHRISTMAS (Book #4)

A CHANCE ENGAGEMENT (Book #5)

A CHANCE DREAM (Book #6)

A CHANCE WEDDING (Book #7)

ENDLESS HARBOR ROMANTIC COMEDY

ALWAYS, WITH YOU (Book #1)

ALWAYS, FOREVER (Book #2)

ALWAYS, PLUS ONE (Book #3)

ALWAYS, TOGETHER (Book #4)

ALWAYS, LIKE THIS (Book #5)

ALWAYS, FATED (Book #6)

ALWAYS, FOR LOVE (Book #7)

ALWAYS, JUST US (Book #8)

ALWAYS, IN LOVE (Book #9)

ELIZA MONTAGU COZY MYSTERY

MURDER AT THE HEDGEROW (Book #1)

A DALLOP OF DEATH (Book #2)

CALAMITY AT THE BALL (Book #3)

A SPEAKEASY DEMISE (Book #4)

A FLAPPER FATALITY (Book #5)
BUMPED BY A DAME (Book #6)
A DOLL'S DEBACLE (Book #7)
A FELLA'S RUIN (Book #8)
A GAL'S OFFING (Book #9)

LACEY DOYLE COZY MYSTERY

MURDER IN THE MANOR (Book#1)
DEATH AND A DOG (Book #2)
CRIME IN THE CAFE (Book #3)
VEXED ON A VISIT (Book #4)
KILLED WITH A KISS (Book #5)
PERISHED BY A PAINTING (Book #6)
SILENCED BY A SPELL (Book #7)
FRAMED BY A FORGERY (Book #8)
CATASTROPHE IN A CLOISTER (Book #9)

TUSCAN VINEYARD COZY MYSTERY

AGED FOR MURDER (Book #1)
AGED FOR DEATH (Book #2)
AGED FOR MAYHEM (Book #3)
AGED FOR SEDUCTION (Book #4)
AGED FOR VENGEANCE (Book #5)
AGED FOR ACRIMONY (Book #6)
AGED FOR MALICE (Book #7)

DUBIOUS WITCH COZY MYSTERY

SKEPTIC IN SALEM: AN EPISODE OF MURDER (Book #1)
SKEPTIC IN SALEM: AN EPISODE OF CRIME (Book #2)
SKEPTIC IN SALEM: AN EPISODE OF DEATH (Book #3)

BEACHFRONT BAKERY COZY MYSTERY

BEACHFRONT BAKERY: A KILLER CUPCAKE (Book #1)
BEACHFRONT BAKERY: A MURDEROUS MACARON (Book #2)
BEACHFRONT BAKERY: A PERILOUS CAKE POP (Book #3)
BEACHFRONT BAKERY: A DEADLY DANISH (Book #4)
BEACHFRONT BAKERY: A TREACHEROUS TART (Book #5)
BEACHFRONT BAKERY: A CALAMITOUS COOKIE (Book #6)

CATS AND DOGS COZY MYSTERY

A VILLA IN SICILY: OLIVE OIL AND MURDER (Book #1)
A VILLA IN SICILY: FIGS AND A CADAVER (Book #2)
A VILLA IN SICILY: VINO AND DEATH (Book #3)
A VILLA IN SICILY: CAPERS AND CALAMITY (Book #4)
A VILLA IN SICILY: ORANGE GROVES AND VENGEANCE (Book #5)
A VILLA IN SICILY: CANNOLI AND A CASUALTY (Book #6)

ALICE BLOOM COZY MYSTERY

MURDER IN THE MARIGOLDS (Book #1)
RUIN IN THE ROSES (Book #2)
DECEIT IN THE DAFFODILS (Book #3)
SCANDAL IN THE SAFFRON (Book #4)
CATASTROPHE IN THE CARNATIONS (Book #5)

Made in United States
Cleveland, OH
05 February 2025

14086759R00090